PROMISES TO KEEP

PROMISES TO KEEP

CHARLES DE LINT

Subterranean Press 2007

First Edition

ISBN
978-1-59606-126-2

Subterranean Press
PO Box 190106
Burton, MI 48519

www.subterraneanpress.com

for Andrew & Alice
always on the front lines

Friends are relatives you make for yourself.
—Eustache Deschamps

Everything works out in the end.
If it hasn't worked out, it's not
the end.
—anonymous

Belief's a funny old thing.

When the old maps said "Here there be dragons," for a lot of people that was a serious concern and as good a reason as any to stay right where you were, safe in your own little town or hamlet. Because you knew dragons were waiting for you if you were foolish enough to fare into the unknown—those mysterious regions that lie on the edges of maps, beyond the borders of what is known, or at least what the cartographers know.

And if you did confront a dragon, it would fry you to a crisp with one fiery breath. Unless you were someone like St. George, I suppose, who, by all accounts, actively went out looking for them.

On the other hand, if you didn't believe in those dragons, you probably wouldn't find them if you went wandering off into their territory. For you, they wouldn't be there at all.

That is, unless someone convinced you otherwise…

-1-

Newford, 1972

"Hey, J.C.!" a voice calls as I'm about to cross the street. I'm ready to ignore it until the woman adds, "Jillian Carter!"

It's a name I haven't heard in a long time and all the skin at the nape of my neck tightens in unhappy anticipation and nervousness. I thought I'd managed to put that name behind me now, along with the memories of foster homes and living on the street.

I turn slowly to see a young woman around my age, leaning against the seat of a motorcycle that looks way too big for her. She has a cute black pageboy haircut and tattoos everywhere her skin is showing except for on her face and the back of her hands. A cigarette dangles from glossy red lips, James Dean style. She's wearing tight faded jeans tucked into clunky black motorcycle boots and a jean vest.

"Donna?" I say.

She takes a last drag from her cigarette and flicks the butt to the sidewalk.

"In the flesh, J.C.," she says, then she steps over and gives me a hug.

We're both small women, but her boots give her more height and she's certainly better endowed than I'll ever be unless I get implants. She's never needed them.

"It's been a long time," I say when we step apart.

"Tell me about it."

Donna Birch and I met in Tyson County's Home for Wayward Girls, way back when. And later, the last time I ran away from a foster home, we shared a squat in the Tombs until I took up with this guy named Rob and started crashing with him. But Donna and I still hung out together, and we might have kept it up for years, except she got busted for assaulting some guy in a bar and pulled a year-and-a-day in county, while my life spiraled down into a black hole of heroin and prostitution. We just never connected again.

"You look good," she says.

"I feel good. I've been clean for a couple of years now."

"That'll do it. What else have you been up to?"

"I'm going to art school."

"No shit? I always knew you had it in you. I still have a couple of those little drawings of yours that I rescued from the corner of some squat or other."

"Oh, god."

"No, they're cool. Really." She smiles. "I've cleaned up my act, too. I'm a vegetarian now. My only vice is nicotine, and the odd beer."

"How odd is the beer you drink?"

"Ha ha. No, seriously. I'm done with the drugs and the binge drinking. Been clean for almost a year now myself. You're looking at a whole new Donna Birch."

"I'll say. When did you get into the tattoos?"

She grins. "They tell the story of my life, girl."

She turns and lifts her hair to show me a small one in black and white at the nape of her neck. It's of some little creature that looks like a pair of eyes staring out of a bundle of twigs.

"Remember that?" she asks.

I nod my head because I do. I used to draw that little guy all the time.

"Every one of my tats is a chapter of my life," she says.

She shows off her right bicep where a woman with her page boy hair and a tight red mini-dress is wrapped in barbed-wire that goes on to trail down and around her elbow. Then she turns so that I can see her other bicep where the same woman is playing a stand-up bass, standing on it like a rockabilly queen.

"I'm in a band," she says.

"Where, let me guess. You play stand-up bass."

"Ask me how much I love it."

I smile. "How much do you love it?"

"I could marry it."

"And do you play out at all?" I ask.

That's an expression I got from my friend Geordie who works part-time at the post office with me. This is our second year at it—we met while we were both in training for the upcoming Christmas rush, and don't you know it, it's that time of year again already. It may only be two major holidays away, but before you know it, Halloween and Thanksgiving will be done and we'll be swamped with parcels and cards. The difference this year is that we don't get paid while we're being trained—we just go right to work because we already know the job.

"All the time," Donna says. "We mostly do gigs at stock car races and hot rod shows because that's where the work is for the kind of rockabilly stuff we do. But we play clubs, too, like the one we're at this weekend, right here in town. You ever go to a place called Your Second Home?"

I nod.

"Well, we're playing at Cool Hand's Juke—just down the street from it."

"What's the name of your band?" I ask.

"Big Earl and His Girls. Earl's our frontman—a seriously hot guitar slinger and a decent singer. His wife Lucy plays drums, and I'm...well..."

She turns again so that I can see the bicep with the bass-player tattoo.

"You should come see us," she says. "I'll put you on the guest list."

"I'd like that. Can I bring a friend?"

"Anybody you like." But then she cocks her head and adds, "You're not still with that asswipe Rob are you?"

"No, but sadly, since then there've been other losers almost as charming."

"Isn't that the sorry truth. These days I just tell the guys hitting on me that I'm a big ol' dyke and don't swing their way."

"Big?" I say. "It's only those boots that are making you taller than me."

"I could still whup your ass."

"You wish."

"It's good to see you full of sass again. That last time…"

The last time I saw her I was stumbling down one of those seedy streets that run off Palm, jonesing for a fix.

"It's good to see you, too," I tell her. "Really good. There's not many people from those old days I could say that about. In fact, you're the only one I could say that about."

"Same deal for me, J.C. Same deal for me."

Okay, this is a bit awkward, I realize, but I have to tell her if she's putting my name on the guest list.

"One, um, thing," I say. "I don't really go by Jillian Carter anymore."

She raises an eyebrow.

"It's Jilly Coppercorn now."

She smiles. "That's cool—it still comes out as J.C."

"I guess it does."

"Later," she says. "And you better show tomorrow night, or I'll come looking for you."

"I'll be there."

It's not till she turns toward her bike that I realize the crest on the back of her jean vest are actually gang colours. It's not the Devil's Dragon emblem, which is our local bike gang. This one's got a skull with a patch over one eye socket and flames all around it. Under it are the words "The Pirates."

"This club," I ask. "Is it a biker bar?"

She looks at me over her shoulder. "Don't worry. It'll be cool. Didn't I always take care of you?"

"Until you went to jail."

"Yeah, but I'm a good girl now."

I have to laugh. "Donna, you look like anything *but* a good girl."

"All depends on your definition, J.C."

"I have a gig this weekend," Geordie says when I tell him about Donna's invitation, "so I can't go." He pauses, then adds, "And I hate to tell you this, but there's no such club on either Lee or Gracie."

"Says you."

He smiles. "I've played Your Second Home. I've killed time between sets walking up and down both Lee Street and Gracie, and I never saw a biker bar called Cool Hand's Juke—and I think I'd remember, because it's a great name for a club. And then there's the whole biker thing. Big motorcycles, lined up along the curb. Kind of hard to miss."

"And when exactly, Geordie me lad, was the last time you were up there?"

He shrugs. "A couple of weeks, maybe a month, ago."

"So, maybe it just opened recently. I mean, why would Donna invite me to a club that doesn't exist?"

"I'm the last person you should ask about why people do the kinds of things they do. Surely, you've figured that out by now."

I laugh. It's true that we've not known each for very long, but we seemed to instantly *know* each other, from the first time we met. I can't remember the last time I was comfortable enough with a guy to just hang out with him in his apartment and not be uneasy. Because, as I told Donna, I don't exactly have the best track record when it comes to boyfriends.

Though Geordie's not my boyfriend. He's just a friend who happens to be a boy. Obviously, *that's* the difference.

It's Halloween night, but we don't have parties to go to. We don't need to go anywhere. We've been sitting on the carpet in front of his stereo, listening to records. Sometimes he plunks along quietly on his fiddle, using his thumb for a pick, instead of bowing it. I've been practicing my life-drawing exercises using his hands as models because my sense of perspective sucks. I concentrate on the negative space the way I've been told to in class, but I'm still having trouble with it. Hence, the practice.

Finally, I put my sketchbook aside on the carpet, then lie back and lay my head on it as well. Ceilings are funny things. We hardly ever look up at them.

"Did you know that you have cracks in the plaster around your light fixture?" I say.

"Did you know that this is a crap apartment, so I'm surprised that the whole ceiling hasn't fallen in by now?"

I lift my head enough to look at him.

"I *love* your apartment," I say.

He smiles. "Yes, living in a rooming house will do that."

I decide that the only suitable response to that is to stick out my tongue at him, so I do.

"You know, it's not that late," he says. "We could hike up there and have a look for that club ourselves."

I sit up and shake my head. "No, no. We can't do that."

"Of course not," he says. "That would be the sensible thing to do."

"I," I tell him, paraphrasing what he told me earlier, "am the last person you should consider sensible."

He smiles. "I know. So why shouldn't we go have a look for this club?"

"Because, Geordie me lad, it's kind of a Schrödinger's cat thing. Until I actually go on Friday night, the club has as much chance of existing as not. I like to think that if Donna invited me to see her band on Friday night, then on Friday night that club will be there, even if it's not there right now."

"But you don't want to check it out before that."

"Absolutely not."

"Okay," he says. "I'm not going to even try to understand. But I am curious about why would your friend Donna do this."

"Do what?"

"Send you off to a non-existent club in Lower Foxville."

"It's only a *potentially* non-existent club."

"You know what I mean."

I shrug. "She's always been a bit odd. She was like that from the first time we met."

"I shudder to think of the sort of person you would call odd."

"Did I mention the tattoos?"

He nods. "And the Bettie Page hair and the motorcycle."

"So you see, the conundrum of a club that might or might not exist fits right in."

"I don't, you know. See, I mean."

"You only think you don't," I tell him. "But you're right. She's not terribly odd. Really odd would be if she had snakes for hair, or if she carried a trident and had a voice so deep that the foundations of buildings would shake when she speaks."

"That would definitely fit my concept of odd."

"Or," I go on, warming to my subject, "if whenever she sings and she hits this particularly high note, a golden egg would plop out of her bum."

Geordie pulls a face. "Now I have to get that image out of my head."

"She has a nice bum," I tell him. "You'd like it."

"How'd the two of you meet?" he asks.

-2-

I'd just been kicked out of my second foster home, so that would make it the third time I was escorted to Tyson County's most outdated civic structure: the Home for Wayward Girls. It was a tall, grey-stoned, Gothic monstrosity of a building that used to be a convent until the Catholic Church sold it off and social services took it over. The place had about as much warmth and charm as the sour-faced matron who was its warden—excuse me, I mean its head-mistress, since that's how Miss Hallworth insisted on being addressed. The Home wasn't quite juvie, but it wasn't a happy place by any stretch of the imagination.

I'd just turned thirteen when I was marched into the long dormitory that was to be my new home until some other family could be found to foster me. Or should I say, cash the cheques they got for taking in kids that they'd then use as slave labour, or worse. I'm not saying all foster parents are like that; but the ones I got sure were.

The dorms in the Home had ten beds to a room, five along either wall with a small combination dresser/night table between each, in which we could store our clothing and meager possessions. No one kept anything of value in them—anything not nailed down in that place was immediately stolen.

There was one other girl in the dorm when I was being shown my bed and where to store my stuff, and that was Donna. She already had her bangs back then, but her black hair was longer and pulled back into a pony-tail. She was dressed all in black—T-shirt, jeans, big clunky shoes—and this was back before the whole Goth thing had ever started.

I don't know why we hit it off the way we did. I wasn't exactly what you'd call a people person in those days, and I found out later that Donna had walls between herself and the world that were as tall and thick as mine.

But as soon as the social worker left the dorm, Donna came over and sat on the end of my bed. I stiffened immediately. Like I said, I'd been here twice before. I knew from experience that the girls in this place could be divided into two groups: those who just wanted to be left alone, and those who were out to take advantage of anyone and anything they could.

"Hey," she said.

I turned to her, schooling my features to be impassive. I didn't want to look like a victim, but I sure didn't want to look like I was hoping to be her friend, either. I'd seen too many girls in here, thinking they'd found a friend, only to end up getting screwed over, one way or another. You might have to do the other girl's chores—make her bed, do her laundry, do her homework—or you could end up turning tricks in the exercise yard, blowing guys through the chain link fence while your "friend" collects the money.

"Look," I said. "I don't have any smokes, candy or make-up, and I sure as hell don't have any jewelry."

She smiled. "And your point is?"

"I don't have anything you might want."

"How do you know what I want?"

"This isn't my first time here."

"Donna," she said.

"What?"

"My name's Donna Birch."

She held out her hand, and reluctantly, I reached over to shake.

"I'm Jillian Carter."

She nodded. "Yeah, I know. My brother told me to look for you today. He said you'd be the only person I could trust in here."

"Your…brother…"

She nodded again. "Tommy, yeah. I doubt you know him."

"If we've never met, why would he tell you that?"

"Oh well…you know how it is."

"Actually, I don't," I said. "I don't know *what* you're talking about."

But instead of explaining herself, she changed the subject.

"Do you ever wonder what happens after you die?" she asked.

"Sure. I guess."

"Not everybody goes on. Some of the dead hang around to look after their loved ones. Problem is, most people can't hear or see them, so that makes it a little hard on the dead."

Now she was starting to creep me out. I didn't know what her game was, but I thought I could see where this conversation was going.

"And you're one of those people," I said, "who can see the ghosts of dead people."

"Bingo."

"And I suppose your brother's dead."

"A year ago," she said. "The old man came home from a night of binge drinking and shot us all—Mom, Tommy and me—before he turned the gun on himself."

She lifted her shirt and I saw the puckered scar in the middle of her chest, just below her bra.

"The dying part," she said, "it didn't really take with me. Oh, I saw the white light and everything, but something—Tommy says it was him—kept pushing me back. And then I woke up in a hospital bed to find myself a ward of the state."

"God…"

"Oh, I don't think God was much involved in any of it."

"No, I mean…"

"Yeah, I know. It's freaky weird, isn't it?"

"I was going to say I'm sorry."

She gave me a slow nod. "See, Tommy was right. I didn't want to tell you any of this—it's not something I particularly want broadcast around—but he said you'd be cool. He said you'd understand."

"Yeah, well, I understand weird-ass families, that's for sure."

She smiled. "And when I tell you about how I talk to the dead, you don't even blink an eye."

"I…"

As soon as she said it, I realized that I hadn't. She'd told me about her dead brother talking to her and I didn't even think to call her on it.

Now, I've always had an active imagination. When I was a kid, I talked to trees and liked to pretend that the characters in my fairy tale books were real. In my head, they had all sorts of adventures outside of the pages of their storybooks. But it was all just that: imagination. The trees never talked back to me. The fairy tale characters stayed in my head.

While I wasn't that little kid any more, I still liked to daydream about all sorts of improbable, magical things. But I hadn't actually experienced anything. I'd never met anybody who had—or who would, at least, admit to it. And why would they? The real world didn't have magic and ghosts and fairies wandering about in it.

I knew that. Everybody knew that.

So it was weird that I hadn't called her on it. And I still had no urge to do so now.

Worse, I found myself liking her. Trusting her, even.

In this place, that was a sure recipe for disaster.

"Why didn't I?" I said.

It wasn't until Donna answered that I realized I'd spoken aloud.

"Why didn't you what?" she asked. "Blink an eye?"

I nodded.

"Maybe it's because you've got a generous heart and you know that I need your support in this place as much as you need mine."

"I told you. This isn't my first time in here. I got through it."

"Yeah, but were you ever happy?"

"I'm never happy," I said.

She grinned. "So maybe that's going to change now."

She digs in her pocket and comes up with a packet of gum.

"You want a piece?" she asked.

There hadn't been many changes since my last stint in the Home for Wayward Girls. Miss Hallworth was still in charge, her employees were as dour-faced and unpleasant as they ever were, and the place was still a gloomy mausoleum. The big difference was that the older girls who'd been running the show the last time I was here had been replaced by ones a year or so younger than Connie Hayes and her gang. The new queen bee was Shannon Pierce—a redhead where Connie had been blonde, but otherwise they were cut from the same cloth.

I managed to stay out of her way, if not off her radar, for most of the day. But just before bedtime, she and a couple of her girls caught me alone in the communal bathroom. My heart sank when I looked up from the sink to see Shannon reflected in my mirror. She was standing right behind me. A black girl named Linda lounged against the wall by the paper dispenser. The third of the threesome was Anna Louise, a brunette wearing lipstick the colour of fresh blood and way too much eye shadow.

Shannon lit a cigarette—a big no-no, so far as the staff here were concerned, but I wasn't about to say anything about it.

"So," she said. "You're the new girl."

I turned from the sink and nodded.

"Though not so new," I said. "This is my third time in here."

Shannon arched her brows and blew out a stream of smoke. "Is that supposed to impress me?"

I shook my head. It didn't matter what I said or did, I knew how this was going to end. I just hoped they'd be satisfied with a few punches and kicks, and that no bones would be broken. I could have mouthed off. I could be less passive. But outnumbered three-to-one, that would only make it worse.

I hated being the victim, but I was coming to understand that that's what I was. In my own family. In the foster homes I'd been put in. Out on the street, in this place, or anywhere at all. I was always small, never strong, and people tended to take advantage of me just because they could. That was the way the world worked. *The Bible* might say that the meek would inherit the earth, but if we ever did, we'd be so bruised and battered by that time, we wouldn't be able to do anything with it.

"We checked your night table," Shannon went on, "and it was empty except for some stupid book."

I didn't say anything.

"So where's your stash, new girl? What've you got? Smokes? Dope? Some cash?"

I was about to answer when I saw Donna appear in the doorway. Shannon hadn't noticed her yet, but Linda straightened from the wall where she'd been lounging.

"Hey, a party!" Donna said in a bright voice. "And no one thought to invite me."

"Piss off, Birch," Anna Louise told her.

But Donna ignored her.

"You guys ever hear of razor-bombs?" she asked. "They're the coolest things. You just chew up a big wad of gum, stick it full of blades, then slip it into somebody's bed while they're sleeping. First move they make and there's blood everywhere."

Shannon turned to look at her. "What the hell are you on about?"

"It works best if you throw two or three of them into the bed, and then pull the fire alarm."

I couldn't see Shannon's face, but I knew she was scowling.

"Are you threatening us?" she said, her voice grim.

"Now why would I do that?"

Oh, please just go away, I thought. Don't try to rescue me. That's just going to make it worse for both of us.

But it wasn't as though Donna could read my mind. She wasn't even looking at me.

"Just stay out of this, twerp," Shannon told her. "Unless you want your head kicked in, too."

"Well, you'd better make sure you kill me," Donna said, "because you and your little friends need to sleep sometime and like I said, those razor-bombs, they'll make a mess of a pretty girl like you. Or maybe you'll wake up to find someone sticking a hypodermic needle into your neck—send you on a trip that you'll never come back from."

Shannon shook her head. "See, now you're just pissing me off. Somebody grab her."

When Linda and Anna Louise moved forward, Donna stretched out her arms like she was ready for her cross.

"Yeah, that's right," she said. "Come on and grab me. Get on my list."

The other two girls hesitated, looking to Shannon.

"You ever wonder what I'm doing in here?" Donna asked. "You should ask my family—oh wait. You can't. Because they're all dead."

"You never killed them," Shannon said.

But I could hear the uncertainty in her voice.

"So you know that for a fact?" Donna asked. She lowered her arms. "Here's the deal," she added, "and I'm only going to make this offer once. You leave us alone, we'll leave you alone. It's as simple as that. No one has to know what went down in here. So far as the other girls are concerned, we'll be living in your shadow, just as they are. But I swear, if you or *anybody* comes after us, you'd damn well better make sure you kill me, because I never forget, and I sure don't forgive."

"Yeah?" Shannon said. "And what do we get out of this?"

Donna smiled and I felt a shiver go up my spine at the weird light in her eyes. It was like she *wanted* them to start something.

"You get to live," she said.

It was so quiet in there that all I could hear was our breathing. The drip from one of the shower heads. A gurgle from the holding tank of one of the toilets. Then Shannon shrugged.

"Screw this," she said. "But this isn't over, Birch."

Donna stayed in the doorway, blocking their exit.

"No," she said. "You're misunderstanding me. This is totally over. Or you start it right now, and if you don't kill me, I finish it."

The two of them faced each other until Shannon nodded.

"Okay," she said. "It's over."

Donna studied her face for a long moment, then finally stepped aside.

I sank to the floor as Shannon and her friends left the bathroom. I had to hold my arms across my chest and lean my head against one of the pipes under the sink. I had the shakes and all I could do was repeat, "Oh my god, oh my god." Over and over again. When Donna knelt in front of me and reached out a hand, I couldn't help it. I flinched.

"It's just me," she said, her voice soft, the weird light gone from her eyes.

"You…you said your father…"

"He did. That was just talk. I needed to freak them out."

"Yeah, well…you…you sure freaked me out."

"I'm sorry, J.C., but I had to do something. They were really going to hurt you—I heard them talking."

"So you'd never…"

Something went hard in her eyes.

"Oh, that part was true," she said, her voice flat. "Nobody's ever going to scare me again. They can hurt me. They can beat me black and blue, or even kill me. But they can't scare me."

"How…how did you get so brave?"

Her eyes softened, went sad.

"I'm not brave," she said. "I just don't care anymore."

I really didn't think Shannon and her friends would leave it at that, but they must have seen what I saw in Donna's eyes, and they just ignored us from that night on. So the rest of my stay at the home was pretty uneventful this time out. I went to classes and hung out with Donna. Some of the girls thought we were lesbians, but we didn't care. Others called us the Psycho Twins, and Donna liked that. I just thought, let them think whatever they wanted, so long as they leave us alone.

This was all so new for me. Not the girls making snarky comments—I'd been there way too many times before. No, I'd just never had a friend before—I mean, a real friend. Someone I could actually count on. It was a novel, exhilarating experience for me. We talked about everything, and all the walls between us and the world came down when it was just the two of us.

And there was something else. When Donna was with me, I didn't feel so much like a victim anymore. I felt like I actually had some worth, in and of myself. I'd never known before how much a difference it could make having even just one person believe in me.

The only weird thing was how sometimes I'd see Donna sitting up in her bed, or standing in the corner of the exercise yard, talking to herself. She looked just as though she was having a conversation, pausing as though listening to some invisible person, then nodding, or interjecting a comment.

I didn't ask her about it for the longest time—probably because I already knew how she'd answer and I wasn't sure how I felt about that answer. When finally I did, she just smiled at me.

"I was wondering how long it'd take you," she said.

"I don't mean to pry."

She shook her head. "You can ask me anything you want, J.C. You know that. We don't have secrets, right?"

"I guess."

"But this thing you're asking me, you already know who I'm talking to."

"Your brother."

There. I'd said the impossible words.

"I guess you think it's weird, or scary," she said, "but it's cool. Really. I know you came from a crap family, but brothers aren't all like your brother Del. You'd have liked Tommy. And let me tell you, if we'd known you while Tommy was still alive, your Del'd be walking around on crutches…if he was walking around at all."

"So you can really talk to him."

She nodded.

"And…are there others you can, you know, talk to?"

"I guess there must be, but it's only Tommy who comes to me. And I know what you're thinking: maybe this is all just in my head. Maybe I'm just making him up because I miss him so much."

"I wasn't thinking that."

"Bull, you weren't."

"Okay, maybe a little."

"Well, I don't blame you," she said. "If before this, anyone had come up to me and told me that they can talk to dead people, I'd recommend we get the padded cell ready. But Tommy does talk to me. He told me you were coming and that we'd make a family of our own, here where nobody else wants us. And we have, haven't we?"

I nod.

"So you don't need to worry, J.C. I'm not crazy, and he won't hurt you. I can't promise you much, but I can promise you that."

-3-

I'm working the evening shift at Kathryn's Café with Wendy St.
James. It's Wednesday, which means it's poetry night, so it's not so
busy—for us, I mean. There's a good house, but the audience is mostly
made up of poets who are either going to perform tonight, or those
who've come to check out the competition. They range from lovely to
intense in temperament, but they're not heavy drinkers and most of
them will nurse their tea, coffee, or glass of wine for as long as they can.
I guess they learned the lesson that Dylan Thomas didn't.

"Have you ever heard of a bar called Cool Hand's Juke?" I ask
Wendy.

Okay, I may have maintained an air of certainty in front of
Geordie, but the truth is I'm as confused as he was about this whole
does it/does it not exist business. Maybe confused's not quite the right
word. Let's say curious. Not enough to go up and have a look until
Friday night rolls around, but enough to ask about the place.

So far, no one's ever heard of it, which does not bode well except
for this one fact: I know that if Donna said she'd meet me there, she'll
be there. The club will be there.

Wendy and I are both sitting on stools behind the bar when I ask
her the question, leaning on the countertop as a tall young man with
a bird's nest of red hair invokes the ghosts of Ferlinghetti and Gins-
berg from the stage. I mean stylistically, or course, since both those
poets are still very much alive, although they're rapidly becoming part
of the older generation.

Wendy's about my size, with blonde curls instead of my tangle of dark hair. She's one of the small coterie of new friends I've made since I went clean and started my first year at Butler U. She doesn't take any classes with me since her real interest is in the written word.

She shakes her head in response to my question. "No, that's a new one for me. Where is it?"

"Up in Foxville—near Your Second Home."

"Oh, I don't go up there much. The neighbourhood's too rough."

"It's not that bad."

"Says the tough Tyson girl. Why are you asking, anyway?"

"An old friend of mine's in a band that's playing there this weekend."

She makes a question with her eyebrows. "When you say 'old,' do you mean a senior citizen?"

"Ha ha. No, Donna's from my Tyson days."

"I thought you didn't have any friends from back then."

"She's pretty much the only one. We met in the Home for Wayward Girls, then lost touch when she got out ahead of me—she was a year older. We hooked up again when we were both squatting in the Tombs."

"You've lived such a wild life," Wendy says.

"I could have totally done with a boring one."

Wendy shakes her head. "Not you. I don't mean the bad stuff, but you're too full of life to ever settle for anything even close to boring. Is it me," she adds, her gaze going to the stage, "or is this guy totally channeling 'A Coney Island of the Mind'?"

I smile. Wendy can be so polite. Anybody else would have just come out and said he was ripping Ferlinghetti off.

"It's not you," I say.

"I didn't think so."

"You should get up and read some of your own poetry."

"As if. Some of mine actually scans—and worse, it rhymes. This crowd would eat me alive."

I laugh.

"So tell me about this old friend of yours," Wendy says. "How'd you fall out of touch with her?"

The good humour leaves my features.

"I was such a mess in those days," I say.

-4-

"Oh my god," I said as the last person I expected to see in this ragged old excuse for a building appeared in the doorway of my room.

Donna grinned. "Hey, J.C. Long time no see." She gave the room a once over, then added, "Nice digs."

She was teasing me, but that was okay. There were lots of street kids squatting in this old office building on the edge of the Tombs—some runaways, too—but nobody was really taking care of the place, and it had been pretty much already falling down on itself when we moved in. I shared the room I lived in with a couple of other girls: Ellie and Alex. There wasn't much in the way of furnishings. After dragging them in from a room down the hall, we'd laid old metal file cabinets down on their sides in between our mattresses and bedding to create the semblance of privacy. It worked fine, when you were lying down. Ellie had made some brick and plank bookcases on which she stored a collection of dried flowers, bottle caps, and other found objects. I'd used my bricks and planks to make a night table to hold my candle and books.

"It's warm and dry," I said.

"And away from the eyes of social services."

I shrugged. "I made a deal with my last foster parents. They can keep collecting their cheques if they don't rat me out, and I'll keep out of trouble and not rat them out."

"Sweet. So how's keeping out of trouble working out for you?"

"I'm managing a low profile."

She laughed. "If your profile got any lower, you wouldn't exist anymore. You need to stand up for yourself more. Didn't you learn anything from me?"

"Only how to get into trouble."

"Now that hurts." She cocked her head and added, "So don't I at least get a hello hug?"

When she stepped away from the doorway, I got up from my mattress and we met in the middle of the room.

"I've really missed you," I told her.

"Me, too. Everybody treat you okay back at the home?"

"They left me alone."

"Well, that's something, right?"

I nodded. "It was enough."

I returned to my mattress and she joined me. Her gaze went to the set of works sitting on the board I was using for a night table. I figured she was going to give me a hard time about it, but all she asked was what I was shooting and if I had any more. I had enough for both of us, so we shot each other up, then laid back on the mattress and got caught up through a cloud of bliss.

Here's the thing about heroin. Yeah, when you're strung out, you're basically shooting up just to stop the sick feeling. You know you're messed up, but it doesn't matter. All you care about is the next hit. But what nobody really talks about is why people get addicted. They don't become junkies because they think there's something cool about the shakes and the puking and the desperate need to get a fix. They become junkies because when you first start, it's just so damn sweet. There's not another high that can compare. And *everybody* can control themselves at first. They do just enough to get that sweet, dreamy buzz.

But somewhere along the line, it turns on you and you stop shooting up to get high. Eventually, it comes to the point where it's, screw getting high. All you're trying to do is survive.

But I wasn't at that point yet, and neither was Donna. We weren't even thinking about it. Like every other about-to-be junkie, we were totally in control of the dope; it wasn't in control of us.

Donna moved into the squat—we got another room down the hall—and it was party central for us, whenever we had the money to score. I'm not sure when it started to go downhill. In retrospect, I guess it was after I started dating Rob.

Donna never liked him, but while I was willing to listen to her about a lot of things, Rob wasn't one of them.

"He's just playing you," she told me the last time we argued about him.

"Why do you say that? He's hot and he digs me—what's so bad about that? Are you mad because he's into me instead of you?"

I remember how sad her eyes got when I said that.

Guys were always going for Donna and you only had to look at her once to know why. She was generously built and carried herself with a natural sexuality that wasn't remotely forced. It was just the way she was.

"You know I'd never stand in the way of your happiness," she said.

"I know. I'm sorry. I shouldn't have said that."

"It's cool. We're just not going to talk about him again—deal?"

"I guess."

But that was when we started to drift apart. I don't know exactly when she went from casual user to junkie, but it couldn't have been long after that. I know it wasn't for me. Everything kind of spiraled out of control and it got to the point where I'd do anything for a fix, and that included letting Rob pimp me out.

The last time I saw Donna, I was so messed up I could barely see straight. Then I heard about her getting into a fight with some straight guy in a bar and my life stumbled into a black hole that it took me a couple of years to climb out of again.

I had help. I couldn't have done it on my own. All the strength it took I borrowed from those around me, except for one little bit, and that was Donna's voice, talking to me out of my memories. Telling me to be strong. That I didn't need to be the victim. That just because people hurt me, it didn't mean they owned me.

So I got past it. The need. The jones.

When I put it like that, it seems so simple. But I had to claw my way out and I know for a fact, I couldn't have done it on my own. Except, in the end, I was the only one who could do it. I was the only one who could make the choice to use, or not. To redo my life, or just give it up to the shadows that were forever crawling around in my head.

I chose to be better.

I chose to be strong.

God knows, it's not always easy, but it's a funny thing. Once it starts to get to be a habit, once you start to define yourself by a new set of needs and desires, the old ones don't have seem to be able to muster as persuasive a hold on you anymore.

I think the biggest change—the thing that really turned it around for me—was that I wasn't scared anymore. I don't know how I got so brave. It certainly wasn't that I didn't care. Actually, I cared *more*. I cared about *everything* and everybody.

Maybe that's what made the difference.

It wasn't me against the world anymore. It was me *connected* to the world, and wanting it to be a good place for everybody.

I know. It's an impossible task. But if nobody makes the effort, if nobody tries to make a difference just around themselves, in their own neighbourhoods, then it's never going to get done, is it?

-5-

So Friday night rolls around and I'm on my own as I walk up to Foxville. I could have taken the bus, I guess, but I had little enough money and I wanted to at least be able to buy Donna and myself a beer, and tip the waitress. Being a poor student sucks, but I can live with it, because when I consider the alternative—where my life was going—well, I probably wouldn't even be alive today, would I?

I don't really mind being on my own. A few years ago, and I'd have been scared. As soon as the day rolled into the night I'd be looking for a place to hide, like a wild animal, needing its den. But things have changed now. I don't think the streets are any safer—probably less so—but somehow going clean also instilled a sense of fearlessness in me. I don't mean I'm totally stupid. I'm careful. I carry a little can of mace in the pocket of my jacket. But I don't avoid the dark streets just because there are freaks out here in the night.

It drives some of my new girlfriends crazy. They take cabs at night, or stay in. But I can't do that, because it means the freaks have won.

I smile as I reach the block that Your Second Home's on. There's a crowd outside, waiting to get in to see a local band doing a Deep Purple tribute show. That's not what makes me smile. A half block up from the club and across the street, I see a line of motorcycles pulled up to the curb. And there, right above them, is a neon sign that reads "Cool Hand's Juke." The name makes less and less sense, the more I think about it, but that doesn't matter. What matters is that it exists.

"Score one for Donna, Geordie me lad," I say.

That gets me an odd look from the closest kids waiting to get into Your Second Home. I just give them a bright smile as I keep going, across the street, right up to the door of Cool Hand's Juke. The doorman's almost as wide as he is tall. He's a great big brute of a man with a ponytail, his biceps and chest straining at the thin fabric of a plain white T-shirt. The clipboard he's holding looks tiny in his meaty hands.

He gives me a once-over.

"I don't think so, kid," he says.

I get this all the time, because of my size. I pull out my I.D. and show it to him. He gives it careful look, then nods.

"That'll be seven bucks," he says.

"I supposed to be on the guest list," I tell him.

He looks at his clipboard and runs a finger down a column of names until it stops on mine.

"Just you?" he asks. "I've got you down here for two."

"It's just me."

He nods. "Yeah, that's probably a smart move, all things considered."

"What do you mean?"

But he doesn't answer me. He just opens the door and waves me down a short hall.

"You should get going," he says. "You're the last to arrive and they were holding the show till you got here."

I give him a blank look. Why would the show be held up until my arrival? And who starts a show this early on a Friday night? It's just turned nine.

"Are you going in, or what?" the doorman asks.

"Sure, I…"

"Just go down the hall—you can't miss it."

I get a strange feeling as I step through the door, like my ears just popped from coming down too fast in an elevator. There's a moment of vertigo with my stomach acting like a high diver doing a series of full body turns before she hits the water. Then it's gone and I hear the music coming from the door of the club down the hall. I smell cigarette smoke and beer, but my stomach stays steady.

I look back at the doorman but he's got his back to me. Okay, that was weird. I wait a beat, just to make sure the vertigo's gone for sure, then shrug and continue down the hallway. I pause in the doorway of the club.

The room's almost full, with a lot of black leather and jeans. But that's mostly the guys. The girls are all in tight dresses and fishnets. Some of them look like they stepped right out of the early sixties with their beehives and ponytails. Others are like Donna, tattooed and a little tough looking. Some of them have multi-coloured hair, and some of *those* have spiked their hair with gel so that it stands up from their head like a rooster's tail feathers.

The music's coming from a sound system, but there are instruments on the stage: a stand-up bass and a small drum kit, guitars and speakers, mike stands with clunky, old-fashioned mikes on them. Geordie would know what kind they are. A drop cloth hangs behind the stage with a mural painted on it depicting a stock car race. The cars are coming right at the stage and are so well-rendered that I have a momentary adrenalin rush, thinking they're real.

Nobody's paying much attention to me until I see Donna, with the same black page boy haircut and tight red dress she has in the tattoo on her arm. She's by a table to the left of the stage, right in front of the dance floor, standing and waving at me, cigarette in her hand. I can tell she's saying something, but I can't make out what over the music and conversation.

I make my way through the tables until we're close enough to hug. Her hair smells good—fresh like a fruit stand—and I want to ask her what kind of shampoo she's using, but she's already stepping back.

"See?" she says. "I told you she'd come."

Then she introduces me to her friends. Big Earl looks pretty much the way I expected—big and round, and cheerful. His wife Lucy's got a blonde beehive and could have been poured into the yellow satiny dress she's wearing. She has heels so high that I can't imagine her working the pedals of her drum kit in them. She must play barefoot.

The other couple are Frank and Sadie. He's a mechanic at a local garage, and a stock car racer, while she's plays on a roller derby team— "I'm tougher than I look," she says when my eyebrows go up. Frank looks positively tiny beside Big Earl, but he's not really a small guy. He's in jeans and a white T-shirt, his dark hair slicked back from his forehead. Sadie's genuinely petite which makes her around my size. Her dress is green—which really sets off her bright red hair—but otherwise it could have come off the same rack as Lucy's.

Though everyone's kind of casual chic, I feel frumpy in my sweater and baggy cotton pants, my mess of tangles only barely tamed into a ponytail. But that's the story of my life. I never fit in.

"This is so cool," Lucy says when we're all sitting down at the table. "Donna's never brought a date to a gig before."

I glance at Donna. She only shrugs, grinning.

"Yeah, well we go way back," I say.

Just like that, I hear some of my old Tyson accent coming back into my voice—that touch of a drawl, with the clip on the hard consonant—and I can't help but smile.

Big Earl nods. "She was saying. You guys first hooked up in juvie or something, right?"

"Or something."

"We've got a real treat tonight," Donna puts in before I can say anything else—like why's she parading all our personal history in front of people who are strangers to me, and what's with the "date" business?

"This is going to be sweet," Frank says.

Big Earl nods and gets up from his seat. He moves easily for such a big guy.

"I'll go tell them she's here," he says, "so we can get the show started."

That seems like the perfect moment for me to find out just what's going on here.

I lean closer to Donna as Big Earl heads off to a door on the other side of the dance floor.

"Okay," I say, "what's with everybody waiting on me?"

"It's no big deal," she says. She reaches across the table and gives my hand a squeeze. "I just wanted to make sure you caught the whole show."

"Yeah, but—"

"Oh, I know. You don't like to be the center of *any* kind of attention. But don't worry. As soon as this acts starts, you're not even going to be thinking about that."

She squeezes my hand again, then turns in her chair as three men amble onto stage. The drummer gets behind the kit. The bass player is carrying an electric bass which he plugs in. The guitarist does the same with his instrument. The crowd starts applauding as he approaches the microphone.

I find myself trying to place him because he looks really familiar. Short wavy hair, those horn-rimmed glasses.

"Hey, great to be here," he says with a Texas accent.

Then they launch into a version of "Peggy Sue" and I twig to the resemblance. Down the street at Your Second Home they've got a Deep Purple tribute happening, but here they have a Buddy Holly look-alike to open the show. He's got an uncanny resemblance to the Lubbock, Texas, pioneer of rock 'n' roll—both in his looks and voice.

I start to settle in my chair to enjoy the show, but then Donna's tugging on my hand, pulling me onto the dance floor. The others at our table are up as well and soon the dance floor's crowded. Halfway through the second number I realize just how much I needed to let off some steam. What with school and work, and then homework, my life seems crammed with things I'm supposed to do. Don't get me wrong—I love that my life has turned around the way it has. But it's hard work and sometimes I just need to relax. Dancing to a great band is a perfect way to do that.

I switch to water after my second beer—I could have had more, even with my limited finances, because nobody will let me pay for my own. It seems I'm on the band's tab. But two's my limit these days. Any more and I start to remember just how easy it is to fall back into the habit of drinking all night, every night. When you're an addict, recovered or not, it's not something you have the luxury to forget. Because for an addict, it doesn't stop there. From drinking beer it's so easy to go to just a couple of puffs from a joint. The next thing you know, you're in a stall in the bathroom, sitting on the toilet and tapping your arm to get a vein to rise.

No thanks.

I love this Buddy Holly tribute band—they know all the songs, and it's such happy music, even when the stories are sad—but I love Donna's band more. It's high energy and loud—sort of rockabilly mixed with a kind of Ventures-twang. Big Earl's got a surprisingly high singing voice, but his guitar growls like he's channeling one of those old surf guitar bands, and the rhythm section is rock-steady and hard-driving.

Even after dancing through a whole set by the opening band, I have to get back onto the dance floor once they start to play. Frank begs off, so it's Sadie and me, dancing with each other, and then with a couple of bikers who are so sweet and not at all the way I expect tough guys that ride with a gang to be.

By the end of the night I should be exhausted, and I am a little tired, but I'm also brimming with energy.

"Somebody needs to take the battery out of that girl," Frank says.

He grins when I give him the finger.

We're sitting at the table with Sadie, watching the band pack up their gear. I offered to help, but they just waved me back to the table, so I pulled out my little sketchbook from the inside pocket of my jacket and drew in it while they worked.

"Big Earl's kind of anal," Sadie confides. "You've got to wrap the cables just so or he's only going to do them all over again himself. It's easier just to leave him to it."

"And besides," Frank adds, "I like to watch people work—don't you?"

"Screw you," Lucy says from the stage where she's dismantling her drum kit and we all laugh.

I can't believe how totally comfortable I feel with these people. Maybe it's being with Donna again, maybe I'm just starting to stretch my wings a little—getting easy in my skin around strangers. I don't know. But I feel relaxed and good. Happy.

I look down at my sketchbook. My sketches are pretty good, if I say so myself. I'm really starting to get the perspective thing—I find it way easier when my subjects are clothed than in life drawing class. The folds in the clothes give me more reference points.

Donna's the first finished and comes to sit beside me. She smiles when she looks at what I'm doing.

"No more fairies and little twig men?" she asks.

"I need to know how to draw from life before I can go back to made-up stuff."

"Maybe your made-up stuff's real somewhere."

I laugh. "Maybe. But I'm here in the real world, so I'm going to learn how to deal with that first."

She gives me a funny look that I can't read, but before I can press her, she asks, "So did you have fun?"

"Totally."

"I've got another surprise for you."

"What is it?"

She shakes her head. "Uh-uh. Then it wouldn't be a surprise, would it? Just stick around a little longer."

"I'm in no hurry to go anywhere."

It's true. I've got homework to do—but it can wait until tomorrow—and my next shift at Kathryn's isn't until the evening, so there's no reason to go home to bed right now. I can catch up on missed sleep tomorrow, along with my homework.

We sit around with the others for awhile longer, joking and laughing. Then Elvis comes on the jukebox, singing "Love Me Tender," and Big Earl and Lucy get up and start to slow dance. A moment later, Frank and Sadie join them.

"That's our cue," Donna says.

She grabs her jacket and we say our goodbyes to the others, before making our way through the tables to leave the club.

"See you later, Ti'Jean," Donna says to the big doorman.

"See you, Donna."

"Ti'Jean is French for Little John," she tells me as we step outside.

"So where's Robin Hood?" I ask.

"Ha ha."

As we step through the door, out onto the pavement, I remember that odd touch of vertigo I got coming in. There's nothing this time, but once we're on the sidewalk, I have a moment of disorientation. You know how it is when you wake up in a strange place, but you forgot that you didn't spend the night in your own bed? How nothing's familiar but you're too sleepy to figure out why?

That's what it's like out on Lee Street right now.

I look around, trying to figure out what's making me feel this way.

"Don't worry," Donna says. She takes my arm and leads me up the street. "You're not crazy. You really are someplace else."

I stop, bringing us both to a halt.

"What are you talking about?" I say.

Except I already know. This isn't Lee Street. This isn't any place I've ever seen before. I'm not even sure it's Newford.

"Where *are* we?" I say.

Donna shrugs. "I don't know what it's called, or even where exactly it is. It's just somewhere else."

"You know you sound—"

"Crazy. Yeah, I know. But here we are all the same."

I look up and down the street. There are stores I don't recognize. Restaurants and other clubs I've never seen before. There aren't any people and there's no vehicular traffic, not even a cab. But it doesn't feel deserted. Everything seems to vibrate with—I don't know. An inner life is the best way I can put it.

"Don't freak," Donna says.

"I'm not freaking—well, not a lot, anyway. I'm just…really confused." I turn to look at her. "What's happening here?"

"You mean 'happened,'" she says. "When you stepped through the front door of the club, you didn't just come into Cool Hand's Juke. You came into a whole other…I don't know. World, I guess."

I remember the feeling I had, going into the club earlier.

"Can…can we get back?" I ask. "To our own world?"

She cocks her head. "You're taking this really well. But then I knew you would."

"You didn't answer me."

"Of course we can go back. I met you there, didn't I?"

I nod. "And you knew I'd take this well because…because Tommy told you?"

"I wondered if you'd remember him."

"It's kind of hard to forget," I say. "You never stopped talking to him, back in the Home."

"Well, that's kind of my surprise," she says.

"I get to finally talk to his ghost?"

"Better. I'm taking you to meet him. And he's not a ghost any-more—not here."

That really stops me—more than the idea of stepping through a club door and landing in some place out of the world ever did.

"Are we—is this the land of the dead?" I ask.

She shakes her head. "I don't think so. It's more a place where ghosts can mingle with living people."

I think back to the club and her band's opening act.

"That was really Buddy Holly, wasn't it?" I say.

She nods.

"God, and he was opening for you!"

"Well, it *was* our gig." She pauses a moment, then adds, "Though we didn't know he was coming by until he showed up at soundcheck and asked if he could play a set."

"You know," I say, "I think I have to sit down on the curb be-cause maybe I'm not taking this so well after all."

Donna helps me sit down. She keeps her arm around my shoul-ders as I put my head between my legs and close my eyes, waiting for the weak, dizzy feeling to go away. I'm not sure how long it is before I finally lift my head again.

"Better?" she asks.

"Maybe. I don't know." I turn to look at her, her face so close to mine. "Do you have any more surprises for me?"

She shakes her head.

"And I'm not dead."

"Not even slightly," she says.

"But we're going to meet your brother."

"Who is dead, yes."

"Oh boy."

I put my head between my legs again.

"This is not a bad thing," Donna says. "It's pretty cool, really. Like I said, I don't know where this city is, but it's a good place. It's not at all like where we came from. There isn't any meanness here and the opportunities are endless. Things just happen the way you want them to. Like you could get an art studio, just like that. To, you know, paint in and everything."

I sit up once more and look across the unfamiliar street for a long moment before I turn back to her.

"Did you ever read *News from Nowhere*?" she asks. "It's by William Morris."

"You mean the Pre-Raphaelite guy?"

She nods.

"I didn't know he wrote books, too," I say.

She laughs. "I didn't know anything about him, but he's a favourite of Tommy's. Anyway, in this book he talks about the perfect place—you know, a utopia."

"Which always goes bad."

"Exactly. But in his book it doesn't because it's the people who change first—inside themselves—instead of somebody laying down a bunch of laws that people have to follow. There's no theft because nobody really owns anything. There's no murder or rape because people just can't imagine doing it. Everybody shares in everything. Sometimes you're, like, digging ditches, or collecting garbage, but it's cool, because it needs to get done and it's good physical work and—well, nobody minds pulling their weight."

"So everything belongs to everyone."

"Kind of," she says.

"And that's what it's like here? All peace, love and flowers?"

"Pretty much."

"So what's with all the bikers?" I ask.

"Oh, that's just our crowd. There's all kinds of people here, from every walk of life. And the bikers are cool here, right? I mean, you were talking and dancing with them. Did they seem heavy to you?"

I shake my head. "No, they were kind of sweet." I look around again, and add, "So where are all the people?"

"I don't know. It's late, so they're probably in bed. For some reason, there's nobody really around on the streets at night."

"This is really, truly weird," I tell her.

"I know. But it's not bad weird."

"I guess not."

"So, are you okay to walk again?"

I nod and we both get up from the curb.

"This is where Tommy and I live," Donna says as she leads me up the steps of an old brownstone.

I pause for a moment at the bottom of the stairs to look around. This is not a fancy neighbourhood. It's nicer than the street my rooming house is on, but it's not high end. The cars parked at the curb are mostly older models—nothing newer than a 1969 Chev two-door a couple of houses down. There's junk at the curb—a stack of boxes spilling newspapers, an old stove with the oven door removed and leaning up against its side. There's no room for gardens, but most of the lower level apartments don't have flower boxes.

"Okay, I don't get it," I say as I join her on the stoop. "If you can have anything you want, why aren't you living someplace fancier?"

"It doesn't work like that," Donna says. "It's more, you find what you need, and we don't need much more than this."

"You make it sounds as though the city's got a mind of its own."

"Maybe it does. I don't know. I just know that when Big Earl and Lucy first brought me here, the only thing I wanted was to see Tommy again, and that's what I got. Tommy, and this place where we can live together like we never could before because…because…"

"Because he died."

She nods.

"But now he's alive again," I say.

"He's alive here."

"Right."

I take a last look down the empty street, then I follow her inside the tenement. There's an old elevator in the foyer, but we take the stairs to their third floor apartment and I finally get to meet Tommy Birch.

He's not at all what I expected. I was thinking, short, slim and dark-haired like his sister, but he looks like he stepped out of an entirely different genetic pool than the one that gave the world Donna. He's tall and well-proportioned, with a head of light brown hair, long and curly, and the kind of dark brown eyes that you just want to fall into.

He's sitting on a sofa in the living room when we come in, reading a book. He puts it aside and gets up.

"Jillian Carter," he says, smiling, with his hand out. "Or should I say Jilly?"

"Jilly's fine," I tell him.

I don't exactly flinch when we shake hands, but I'll admit I thought my hand was going to go right through his, so I'm a little surprised that we can actually clasp hands.

"You thought you couldn't touch me," he says with a smile.

I smile right back. It's hard not to, the way his eyes light up.

"So, what?" I ask. "You're a mind reader, too?"

He shrugs.

"Do you want a beer?" Donna asks me.

"I'd rather have a coffee."

"We only have instant."

I pull a face. "Tea?"

"That I can totally do."

I don't know what we talk about for the next hour or so, but it's comfortable and pleasant, sitting here with the two of them, drinking my tea, laughing at the way they tease each other.

"So, what do you think?" Donna asks when she brings me a second tea.

"About what?"

"Everything. The city. You living in it with us."

"Oh, I don't know…"

"I don't mean right in our apartment, though I'd be totally okay with that if you wanted to."

She looks at her brother, and he nods in agreement.

"But you could get your own place, here in the building," she says, "or wherever you want. You could set up a studio. No more scrambling to make ends meet."

"It seems perfect."

"It *is* perfect." She turns to her brother and adds, "You should lend her that *News from Nowhere* book," before turning back to me.

"It's not like Oz. There's no freaky little wizard, hiding behind a curtain, running the show. It's all totally what we make it."

I nod. "I can tell you love it."

"What's not to love?"

She gives her brother a fond look.

"And what about you?" I ask him.

He shrugs. "It's like Donna says."

"What was it like before?" I ask him. "If you don't mind me bringing it up."

"No, I'm okay talking about it. I remember dying. And I remember pushing Donna back when she tried to follow me into the light. But after that I've got nothing. There's a big hole in my memories—a long space of blankness—and then I was walking down a street in this city, and there Donna was, with Big Earl and Lucy, just coming down the block towards me."

"But you used to talk to her all the time…"

"That's what Donna says. But I don't remember it."

I would hate that, I think. I've had all kinds of crap in my life. There's lots of things I wish had never happened to me. Or that I hadn't done. But I wouldn't want to not remember, because then… then…I'm not sure. I just feel like I wouldn't be who I am today.

I don't know if I'm entirely happy, but I'm working towards it. And I'm strong. And way braver than I was when Donna knew me.

These are things I earned.

"Yeah, it kind of bothers me," Tommy says.

I blink in surprise. "I thought you said you couldn't read minds."

"I don't have to, to know what you're thinking. I have to admit that sometimes, when I'm out, walking around, I get the feeling that everything's a façade. The people I meet, all the buildings, just… everything. And I want to, I don't know, pull down the curtain and see what's really there."

"The wizard with his hands on the gears, making it all work."

"Something like that."

Donna shakes her head. "I don't get you two. This place is a good deal—we don't want for anything. So what's the problem?"

Tommy says the same thing I'm thinking. "That we didn't earn it?"

"No, no. That's old-fashioned thinking. Look at our lives. The messed-up crap that we all had to go through as kids? We earned a break ten times over."

"When you put it like that…" Tommy says.

"What other way is there to put it? Our old man shot us, for Christ's sake. You *died*. And J.C.—we don't even want to start on the hell your brother put you through."

I nod. I might have got past that now. I might have this new life for myself—making friends, attending school. But I still have nightmares.

"Do you really *want* to be dead?" she asks Tommy.

"Not that I remember what it was like, but no."

"Of course you don't. And, J.C. Think of all the years that have already been stolen from you. Other kids were doing the school thing while you were scrabbling to make a living on the street. Is it really so important that you bust your ass to get to the place in your life where you were supposed to be in the first place?"

I shake my head. She's right. But the idea of just turning my back on the world and walking away still feels weird.

"I need to think about this," I say.

"Sure. I get that. There's no deadline. Take your time."

"Maybe I'll talk a walk," I say. "I always think better when I'm moving."

Donna nods. "I remember." Then she smiles and adds, "Well, you don't have to worry about whether or not you'll be safe out on these streets. This place is just like Newford, except without all the bad crap."

"I like Newford," I say, though even I can hear the doubt in my voice.

It's a great city—especially now that I can see more than just its underbelly through a heroin haze. But there are alleys I walk purposefully by, and there are certainly parts of the city I just don't go. I might draw the line in different places than Wendy or our friend Sophie might, but I still draw lines because, while you can be as brave as you like, sometimes you need to be sensible, too.

So now I find myself wondering what it'd be like to have a whole city—"just like Newford," as Donna put it—but where every nook and cranny is open for exploration. I could go out anytime I wanted and just draw, draw, draw to my heart's content.

I've been sitting with my sketchbook on my lap, idly flipping the pages without looking at what I'm doing. Now I glance down and see a double page spread of hand studies.

Geordie's hands.

"I need to think about it," I say again.

"Whatever you need," Donna tells me. "You can find your way back here?"

I nod. "I'm good at finding my way around."

I stuff my sketchbook back into my pocket and stand up. Tommy gives me a casual wave, Donna walks me to the door, and then I'm on my own, making my way down the stairs and out into the city night.

It's quiet out here on the streets, which makes it seem eerie, because back home, the city's never quiet. There's always something going on: cabs trolling the streets for late fares, police cruisers on patrol, one or two people stumbling home from the clubs, or shuffling sleepily off to an early shift at work, sirens in the distance. Here…not so much. There's just me, my footsteps echoing between the buildings because I'm alone on the street and there's nothing to steal away the sound.

But while it's eerie, it's magical, too. It reminds me of the woods outside of Tyson where I grew up, when I'd sneak out in the early morning before anybody else was up, when anything seemed possible. Of course the real word intruded all too soon, but for just that short sweet time, the world was perfect and nothing could harm me.

And it's like that now. I get that same sense of a kindly, watchful presence—some great spirit that wishes everyone and everything well. Maybe Donna's right. Maybe this city does have a spirit, watching over the streets, looking out for us all.

I don't get that feeling in Newford.

I get hints of it. In open lots, and some of the parks, and the narrow alleyways that still have the original cobblestones that were once on all the city streets. But it's never as strong as that spirit in the woods back home. Still, I guess every place has some kind of spirit. It's just harder to sense in some places than it is in others.

But it's not hard here.

I suppose I've walked about twenty blocks before I finally hear some sound of life other than my own footsteps. It's an odd thudding sound that seems familiar. I mean, I've heard it before, but I can't place it—not until I turn down a side street and follow the sound to its source where I discover a pick-up game of basketball in progress. There's a half dozen Latino boys in their late teens/early twenties playing in a school yard and the sound I heard was the ball on the pavement and hitting the board behind the net.

I start to back up the way I've come—because let's face it. A girl alone at night and a bunch of guys? Never a good idea—but I'm too late. The game stops and they all look at me.

"Hey, *chica*!" one of them calls to me. "Are you lost?"

They're walking towards me, a couple in the lead, the rest of them trailing behind, and before I know it, there's no time to turn and run. They're handsome boys, with those dark Spanish good looks, but there's still six of them and only one of me. I put my hand in my pocket and close my fingers around my little can of mace.

"No, I'm good," I say. "I'm just, you know, getting some air."

The one who first spoke nods his head. "Yeah, it's a beautiful night. Are you from around here?"

I'm already shaking my head before I realize I should have just said yes. So now it's a girl on her own who's also a stranger.

"Good," he says. "So we didn't wake you with our game."

"No, I haven't been to bed yet."

"And yet you're looking good."

Why did I have to mention the word "bed"?

"Yes, well…"

"'scool. I'm just saying, you know?"

Oh, why did I have to play the cat and have this need to satisfy my curiosity? Couldn't I have just made a note to myself—weird thumping sound—and have left it at that?

"Since you're not from around here," he goes on, "let me give you a piece of advice. Stay away from the canal tonight."

"The…canal?"

He nods. "Yeah, it's always full of whispers, but they're working high gear tonight."

"Whispers?"

I find myself reduced to being an echo, but I can't seem to help it.

He cocks his head. "You know. The voices repeating what people think of us, though it's never for true, because it all gets changed somewhere between the old world and this one. There's usually just a few of them, drifting on the water like smoke, but it's thick as fog tonight."

"That's why we're here," another of the boys says. He jerks his head in the direction of a boy standing behind him and adds, "Petey got too close and we're trying to get his mind off the crap they were saying."

"I have no idea what you're talking about," I tell them.

The first boy laughs. "You really *are* new, aren't you?"

I find myself relaxing and I let go of the mace, though I don't take my hand out of my pocket. These boys don't seem to mean me any harm. It's weird that they're so friendly—no question—but they don't feel dangerous. Unless muggers in this city chat you up first.

"So explain it to me," I say, adding "*por favor*," which is about the extent of my Spanish.

"Where do you need me to start?" the first boy asks.

"I don't know. How about, where are we, and where are all the other people?"

The boys laugh.

"It's five in the morning," one of the others says.

The first boy nods. "People are sleeping."

"*Everybody?*"

"Except for you and us."

"But there aren't cabs, or police cars. Shouldn't there still be some people going to work, or coming home from a club or something? It's Friday night."

The first boy shrugs. "I guess that's the funny thing about being dead—you sleep more than you did when you were alive."

"Dead?"

I'm sure I didn't hear him right.

The boy cocks his head again, dark eyes studying me.

"Except you're not, are you?" he says.

I'm still hung up on the word "dead." I know. Donna told me all about it, and then there's Tommy, back there in the apartment, and Buddy Holly on stage, earlier this evening. But for some reason, I just stopped thinking about it. Like it wasn't real. Like it was all just Donna talking.

"So…is this heaven or something?" I say.

"Or something. It's some kind of a place on the other side of life, but it's not where most of the dead go. Nobody knows why some of us end up here and some go on, though the old men can go on for hours about it if you make the mistake of asking them."

"I'm having trouble processing this."

"Yeah, everybody's got questions when they first get here, but after awhile, it doesn't seem so important and you just get on with the business of living." He smiles. "Or not living. Whatever. You know what I mean."

I don't, but I nod my head in agreement anyway.

"So you're all…dead?" I ask.

He nods. "Petey and Vito were on the wrong end of a drive-by. Carlos had himself a head-on with an eighteen-wheeler up on Highway 14 that flattened a seriously sweet ride as well as getting himself killed. Bernie ODed, the asshole. And Eddie got shot by a pissed-off boyfriend."

He points out each of them as he tells me their fate.

"And you?" I have to ask.

"Cholo got himself knifed by some Anglos," Carlos says.

"Being the Good Samaritan," Vito adds.

"I was just trying to break up a fight," Cholo says. "It was no big deal."

"Except it got you killed," I say.

Cholo nods. "Yeah, and here we are where we're dead, and you're not."

"I can't believe I'm having this conversation," I tell him.

"Deal," he says. "How'd you get here anyway?"

"I thought I was just going to see a band at a club…"

He laughs. "And it turned out to be a doorway into a whole other world."

"Something like that."

"I guess it happens. But you're the first living person I've met here. I know there are supposed to be others, but I've never met any."

"There was that guy with the clown make-up," Vito puts in.

Cholo smiles. "Yeah, but he was just psycho. Our girl here isn't straitjacket material." That dark gaze of his fixes on me. "Are you?"

"I hope not. But right now, I'm not so sure."

"Oh, this is real. So are you looking for the club that brought you here?"

"Not really. I just wanted to walk around and get a feel of the place."

"Well, that's a good thing," he says. "You wouldn't have found the club anyway, and even if you had, the doorway wouldn't be there anymore."

"What do you mean?"

"Word is, when you find one doorway in, you need to find another to go out again."

"Great."

I'm about to say more, but Petey starts bouncing the basketball on the pavement.

"Are we about done here?" he asks. "Because I've got all these… you know…"

Cholo nods. "Whispers in your head. Yeah, I know. You guys go ahead and play and gimme a few more minutes here."

The boys head back to the basketball hoop and Cholo returns his attention to me.

"I wouldn't think words would trouble a guy like that," I say as I watch them go. "Petey—you all—look tougher than that."

"It's got nothing to do with toughness," Cholo tells me. "Those whispers…they get into your head and keep multiplying until you think you're going crazy. Hell, you could go crazy unless you get your mind on something until they finally wear off."

"So this place isn't perfect," I say. "My friend Donna—she's the one that brought me here—was making out like it was."

"It's sweet, no question."

"But what about these whispers—and this canal you were warning me about?"

"I don't know what to tell you…"

"Jilly," I say, when I realize he's fishing for my name.

"Jilly," he repeats. It's cute, the way my name rolls of his tongue with that accent of his. "Nice. It suits you."

Now he's definitely flirting.

"My real name's Gilbert," he goes on. "Guys back in the neighbourhood, they used to call me Cholo to get a rise out of me, but I just took it for my own, you know? I'm no gangbanger."

"I should get back to my friend's place," I say.

"You sure? I could, you know, show you around."

I smile. "Maybe another time. Do you live around here?"

"Sure. Just ask around. Everybody knows me."

"I will. Thanks for your help."

"*Mucho gusto*," he says. "*Hasta luego*."

I'm not entirely sure what he's saying, but from his smile, I figure it can't be bad.

"Later," I say.

I watch him walk back to where the other boys are playing basketball and smile at the swagger he puts in his walk. I know it's for me. Then I retrace my own steps and head back to Donna and Tommy's apartment.

"We need to talk," I tell Donna when I return.

"Sure. What about?"

I glance at Tommy.

"No offence," I say, 'but could we do this outside?"

Her eyebrows go up, but Tommy just waves a hand, a vague whatever.

We sit out on the stoop and for a few moments we just watch the horizon as it starts to go pink. It's still quiet out here on the city's streets. I remember what Cholo said, about the people not being around because they're sleeping, and it seems odd. I know the whole world's not made up of nightbirds like me, but they're not all morning people either. Why would it be any different here?

"So what's up, J.C.?" Donna finally asks.

I turn to look at her.

"It's not just Tommy, is it?" I say. "It's everybody. This is a city full of dead people."

"Technically, no. I mean, you're here, aren't you?, and you're not dead."

"You know what I mean."

"Who've you been talking to besides me?" she asks.

"That doesn't matter. I just need to know: what's really going on here? Why'd you bring me here?"

She shrugs. "The world never gave you a break. I thought you deserved to be someplace where everything's better."

"And all—okay," I correct myself as she starts to shake her head. "Where most of the people are dead."

"Do they look dead? It's not like I've dragged you into zombieland."

"That's not the point."

"So what is the point?"

"I don't know. Why didn't you tell me about all of this before I came?"

"Would you still have come?"

I have to smile. "Are you forgetting who you're talking to? I'm the one whose prize possession back in the Home was a book of fairy tales. I'm the one always drawing little elves and gremlins on any scrap of paper I can find. Of course I would've come."

"So what's the problem?"

"Is it true—what your brother said?"

"Said about what?"

"That all of this is just a façade. If we could pull back the skin of the world, what would we find?"

"God, I don't know."

"But I can go home—right?"

She nods. "Of course you can. It's just…"

Her voice trails off.

"It's just what?"

"If you go home, you can't come back here. And if you decide to stay here, you can't go home. You get the one chance and that's it. Until you die, I guess."

"You seem to come and go."

She shakes her head.

"Come on, Donna. I met you on a street in Newford. Don't tell me you can't."

"But it's true. Normally I can't. But there's a thing about Halloween that lets you cross back over. I was able to come back that day to see you."

"But we hooked up in the club again, just a few days later..."

My voice trails off as she shakes her head. "I didn't cross over then. You crossed over to here."

"I don't understand," I tell her. "Why do you want me to be here?"

"Like I said, and no lie. I want you to have a good life—the life you never got to have."

"I've *got* a good life. It's not perfect, but it's not crap either. I kicked my habit. I'm finally going to school. I'm making friends."

"I know."

"Then why would you want to take me away from it?"

"I didn't know you were doing okay when I came to see you."

I nod. How could she?

"I don't have some big, evil agenda here," she adds. "I just want to be with the people I love."

"Then why don't you come back with me?" I say. "We could get a bigger place than the room I have in the boarding house. We'd be roomies again."

She shakes her head. "I'm not leaving Tommy."

I know that's true. But I see something else in her eyes, and then I understand something else.

"Oh god," I say. "How did it happen?"

"How did what happen?"

"How did you die? You *can't* come back, can you?"

She shrugs. "It was when I was in county. I pulled that crazy girl routine to get some butch girl to stop bugging me, except she knifed me. Got me four or five times, I guess. I might still have made it, except the guards didn't find me until hours later and by then it was too late. They got me an ambulance, but I died on the way to the hospital."

I put my hand over hers. "That's so horrible."

"I guess. I mean, yeah, at the time. But I'm good now, see?" She pulls back and lifts her top to show me a smooth belly. "Not a mark left on me from it. Even my old bullet scar is gone."

I think about her brother. He was older than her when he died, but now she's older.

"So do you just stay the age you were when you died?" I ask. "Like, forever?"

"I don't know. I guess."

I wonder if I would, being a living person, but I don't ask.

"So tell me you'll stay," Donna says.

"I don't know. You know me. I don't like taking what I haven't earned."

"Well, stay for today, at least. Let me show you around before you make up your mind. It's different in the day."

She's right about that. By the time we leave the apartment the next morning to go have some breakfast and real coffee at a local café, the streets are teeming with people. And no, they don't look like zombies. Not any of them. They just look like ordinary people—every size and shape, age and skin colour.

"So everybody's dead," I say.

"You're not," Tommy says.

"You know what I mean."

He nods and turns in his chair to scan the crowd.

Our café's on the edge of a town square. There's a park in the middle with a market set up inside—half produce, half crafts and the kind of antiques and old stuff you'd see at a rummage sale.

"That girl's not dead." Tommy says. "The one with the striped stockings."

I follow the lead of his pointing finger and see a girl in her early twenties. She's tall and dark-haired, wearing a baggy sweater over her stockings.

"But she's not really alive either," he adds.

Donna nods. "She's a dreamer."

I give them a confused look.

"Sometimes people drift here out of their dreams. That girl's really asleep in her bed. It's only her dreaming self that's gone wandering."

"Okay, that's weird," I say.

Tommy laughs. "And a city full of mostly dead people isn't."

I laugh with him.

"Okay, I give up," I say. "It's all weird."

We have an amazing day. We go to a flea market that takes up the whole of the street for two blocks. We walk through the most gorgeous library I've ever been in. We go to not one, but two, art galleries, one of which has a special exhibit on children's book illustrators from the turn of the century.

For lunch, the Birches take me to a Bohemian area that reminds me of Crowsea back home. It's all used book stores and record shops, little galleries, cafés, clubs, and restaurants. There are junk shops and higher end antique stores, and a tattoo parlour—"That's where I got my ink," Donna tells me. On the sidewalk, there are buskers at almost every second corner, and people with little tables, or just a cloth laid out on the pavement, selling everything from jewelry and South American crafts to used books and home made jellies and salsas.

"Ask about studio space," Donna says when we're in one of the art galleries. "Go on. Just to find out."

I shake my head, but then, of course, she does.

"Are you an artist?" the cute guy behind the counter asks, interest in his voice.

Donna jerks a thumb in my direction. "No, my friend is."

He smiles at me. "We've got some extra space in the warehouse where I've got my studio. It's all open space, but some of the other artists use screens, or have hung up canvas, to give themselves a little privacy."

"That's right near our apartment," Donna says when he gives us the address.

"Just tell them you're a friend of Henry's," he says. "And that would be me."

"I'm Jilly," I say and reach over the counter to shakes his hand.

"So maybe I'll see you there?"

"Maybe. Thanks."

Donna nudges me with her elbow when we're back out on the street.

"You see?" she says. "Not only is there studio space, but there's a cute boy there who's obviously interested in you."

"Oh, I don't think so," I say. "He was just being nice."

I look to Tommy for confirmation, but he shakes his head.

"Definitely interested," he says.

We stand at a corner, waiting for a break in the traffic. I look at the crowds of people, many of them carrying shopping bags, some of them in the middle of buying something from a street vendor, or tossing some coins into a busker's open instrument case.

"Where does the money come from?" I ask.

Donna looks confused. "What do you mean?"

"Well, people are buying stuff all around us. Where do they get their money? How am I supposed to pay for the rent on some studio space?"

"You'd get a job," she says.

I have to laugh. "So after you've died, you come here and it's the same thing all over again. You still have to make a living."

Donna nods. "But the difference is, here you do what you want to do. That's what I meant about things just working out. If you've always wanted to—oh, let's say, be a musician like I did. Here, it happens. There's not all this crap that gets in the way of your actually doing something you love."

"What if you don't want to do anything?" I ask. "What if all you want to do is just laze around and not do much of anything?"

"You mean like my brother?"

Tommy gives her an affectionate push on her shoulder.

"Is that what you do?" I ask him.

He shrugs. "I just like reading and walking around and talking to people."

"So how do you make a living?"

"I don't."

"But where do you get your money for rent and food and your books and everything?"

"I don't know. It just works out."

"But if you *want* to work, those jobs are there," Donna says. "Like that guy back there in the art gallery. Have you noticed how everybody in the stores is happy to be doing what they're doing?"

I nod. I had. But I guess I was still looking for what lay behind all of this perfection. What made it actually work.

"What do you know about the canal?" I ask Donna.

"Which one?"

"There's more than one?"

She nods. "This isn't Newford. There are a half dozen here. What do you want to know about canals for?"

"Nothing," I say.

She's so *into* all of this, I don't have the heart to bring her down. So it's all magic. So I can't understand how it all is the way it is. It doesn't change the fact that this city exists. That it's here. That *we're* here.

"It's all just magic," I find myself repeating aloud.

Donna shrugs. "I guess."

I look at her, one more question rising in my head.

"I thought there was always some sort of payment involved," I say. "You know, when it comes to magic. That there were… consequences."

"Except we've already done the consequences."

I give a slow nod. "Yeah. I guess we have."

So I decide to stay.

We crash right after dinner that night because we've been up way too long and we're starting to get stupid from sleeplessness. But the next morning, Donna wakes me up bright and early and after a shower, my borrowing some fresh clothes from her, and then a quick trip to the corner café for coffee and toast, we're knocking on her super's door to see if there are any apartments available in her building.

The superintendent's an older black woman, very tall, with hair so grey it's almost white. There's music coming from the apartment behind her—sort of Caribbean, but with a really steady groove on the bass and drums—and a wonderfully spicy smell of something cooking. Donna introduces her as Mrs. Harrison.

"You're in luck," Mrs. Harrison says. "There's one on the second floor, but there is a problem with it." She doesn't give us chance to ask what. "The last tenant left all her furniture and I haven't had time to get my son come by with his truck to haul it away."

"Furnished is perfect," Donna says after giving me a grin. "Now, Jilly's only just gotten here, so she doesn't have her finances in order yet. Any chance we can defer payment for a few days?"

"You'll vouch for her?"

"Absolutely."

Mrs. Harrison studies me for a moment, then nods.

"Just a moment," she says.

She goes away.

"I like this music," I say to Donna while we're waiting.

She nods. "I think it comes from Jamaica. That's where Mrs. Harrison is from, originally. You should try her jerk chicken. You get a burn in your mouth just looking at it."

"I'll take that as a compliment," Mrs. Harrison says, returning. She hands me a key ring with two brass keys on it. "Here you go. There's a storage area in the basement."

"I can show her where it is," Donna says.

Mrs. Harrison smiles. "Then, welcome to the building, Jilly…"

"Coppercorn," I finish for her. "Jilly Coppercorn."

I shift the keys to my left hand and we shake. We exchange a few more pleasantries, then Donna and I are going back up the stairs, but this time we're going to *my* apartment.

"You see how things just work out?" Donna says.

"No kidding."

"We'll go to the bank this afternoon. You'll probably already have an account with an inheritance deposited in it from some uncle you never even knew you had."

"I doubt that. I can't imagine a Carter ever having any money to leave to anyone."

"Then it'll be something else. You'll see."

I nod, because I do. Obviously, things do just work out here.

The money in my account turns out to be from investments that I never made, but that doesn't faze the bank manager and he brushes off my protests. So I cave. Why not? Everything else is going my way, so why not this?

I make a small withdrawal and then Donna and I go pick up some groceries and toiletries, and stop in at a goodwill because I can't keep borrowing clothes from Donna. For one thing, all her tops are way too big for me. I pick up a handful of pants, T-shirts and a great old retro sweater from the fifties with a poodle on the back. We'd already bought some underwear at the drug store where I got my toiletries.

"Come up for dinner tonight?" Donna asks when we're standing in my hallway, a pile of shopping bags along one wall.

I nod, she gives me a kiss on the cheek, and then I'm alone.

In my own apartment.

In some weird city where most of the people are dead, but you can't tell because they look just like you and me, and they go about their business no differently than we do.

I was raised Catholic. I remember how scared I was about the afterlife. How when I didn't confess what my brother made me do, what the *priest* made me do, I was sure I was going straight to hell.

Instead, this is where you go.

Where some people go, anyway, because one city can't be big enough to hold every person that dies, can it?

I wonder if there's some common denominator between the people who end up living here?

Or maybe it's just more magic.

After awhile I pull out my sketchbook and sit by the window, drawing in it until it gets dark.

After dinner, Donna asks me if I want to come listen to her band rehearse, but I beg off. I also turn down Tommy's invitation to play chess.

"I'm not big on games," I tell him.

"Games?" he says. "Chess isn't a game, it's—"

"An obsession," Donna puts in, which I'm sure isn't what he was going to say.

Tommy laughs.

Donna walks me to the door of my apartment, then goes off to her rehearsal. I'm not there for more than a few minutes before I'm wishing I'd gone with her. It's not that I don't like the apartment—god, anyone would kill for something like this in downtown Newford. High ceilings, beautiful hardwood floors. There's nothing on the walls except for a few hangers for paintings, strategically placed. There's a little balcony off the bedroom and the main room has a huge bay window with a cushioned windowseat and leaded panes. There's a separate kitchen, a dining area, and even a spare room.

I can't imagine the concept of a spare room. That one room is bigger than my whole place is back in Newford.

No, the apartment's perfect. It's just that I have nothing to do. I've put away my few groceries and other purchases. But I don't have any real art supplies—paints, brushes, canvas. I don't have anything to read. I don't know anybody besides Donna and Tommy. I could go back upstairs and visit with Tommy, but he's probably reading by now and I don't want to play chess anyway.

I sit for awhile in the windowseat and flip through my sketchbook. There are a half-dozen pages of the gig the other night and things I've seen since I got here. Earlier in the book are studies of hands and feet, and right near the beginning are a few pages with rough sketches of some places around my neighbourhood.

I feel funny looking at them and it takes me a long time to figure out what it is that I'm feeling because it's not something I've ever felt before. Never had the reason to, because any place I ever lived before, all I wanted to do was escape from it.

I'm homesick.

I never felt that for any of the squats I lived in. Not in the Home for Wayward Girls and the foster homes, and for sure, not the family home in Tyson. I mean, why would I?

But Newford's different, now that I'm an actual citizen. I have my own place to live. I have a job. I go to school. I have friends.

I have to start over again here.

I close the sketchbook and stick it in my pocket, then stand up and stare out the window. My reflection on the glass is familiar, but everything on the other side of the pane is strange and new. I don't know how long I stand there before I finally turn away from the windowseat and leave the apartment.

It's more like a normal city outside on the streets at this time of night. There's plenty of traffic—cabs, buses, cars, even a few delivery vans. There are people, too. Some are walking their dogs. Some are jogging. Everybody seems to have something to do, someplace they're going.

Me, I'm just wandering, walking around to clear my head and get a bit of a feel for my new surroundings. But while I don't have a destination in mind, I end up back at the basketball court where I met Cholo and his friends last night. There are kids playing, others standing around watching, or practicing moves on their skateboards with a makeshift ramp they've set up. I don't recognize any of them.

I take a different route back to the apartment and find myself walking along a long, two-story brick building just as it starts to rain. I duck under the protection offered by the awning above the front door and watch puddles form on the pavement, lifting in a wave of spray as a cab goes by. On the other side of the street, a couple of guys are sharing an umbrella. They cross the street after another car goes by and approach the entrance where I'm standing.

They're both kind of scruffy looking, their jeans splattered with paint, though their jackets are clean. The taller one has very dark hair and a goatee. His companion has short curly brown hair and dark brown eyes with the longest lashes I've ever seen on a guy. They both smile at me.

"Hello," goatee says. "Did someone lock the door?"

I smile. "I have no idea. I'm just getting out of the rain."

"Oh," his friend says. "We thought you might have studio space. There's so many of us in here that it's hard to keep track of everyone."

I turn to look inside and sure enough, I see art on the walls of the foyer—bold and bright paintings, some very powerful charcoal life drawings. There's even a weird sculpture made of old soup cans and bottles.

This must be the place the fellow in the art store was telling me about.

"Do you know a guy named Henry?" I ask as I turn back to the pair.

"Henry Thornburg?" goatee asks. "Of course. His is the space in the far northeast corner with all the very large paintings. He's probably there right now."

His friend nods. "Henry works most evenings."

"And days, when he's not at the art store."

"He's far more dedicated than we are."

"He lives, eats and breathes his art," goatee says.

"Sometimes, literally," his friend says. "Or so it seems. I'm Grayson, by the way," he adds, holding out his hand. "And the reprobate here who's had the one pint too many is my compatriot and brother-in-arms, Jeremy."

"I think I'm doing a fine job of holding my liquor, thank you very much."

"You are, you are," Grayson says. "I'm merely giving the young lady some background information in case you should blurt out something inappropriate as the conversation progresses."

I have to laugh. I don't think either of them's older than me, but they talk like a pair of little old men, misplaced in time.

"I'm Jilly," I tell them. "Do you think it would be okay to come in and see Henry?"

"Of course," Jeremy says. "I can't imagine why not." He pushes on the door and holds it open for me. "After you."

The tin can and bottle sculpture is even more fun close up. I love how the tin cans that make up its body double as message holders for the various artists. Each one has a name tag and more than a few have rolled up pieces of paper stuck into them.

"That's Amelia," Jeremy says. "She's our secretary and receptionist." He leans a little closer to me and adds in a loud stage whisper, "It's rumoured that she and Grayson are partaking in a bit of an office romance."

I glance at Grayson and he gives me a helpless shrug. "What can I say? I'm helpless before her exotic beauty."

"You're just helpless, period," Jeremy says.

"Yes, well," Grayson says. "I think Jilly would rather see Henry than have to listen to any more of your endless gossip. It's this way," he adds to me and he offers me his arm.

I smile and slip my hand in the crook of his arm and let myself be led down a long hallway. Art in every medium and style hang from the walls but we're walking too quickly for me to get a proper look at any of it. And then we step out onto a small platform and are looking into a vast cavern of a room, checker-boarded with squares of lighted areas and dark ones. The lighted areas are where people are working in various media: oil on canvas or board, watercolours, acrylics, sculpture and even a landscape artist working in fabric and thread.

Grayson and Jeremy rhyme off the names of which artist belongs to which space as we go by. The artists that are here tonight are mostly too preoccupied to look up when we go by, but those who aren't smile and exchange a few words with my companions after giving me a friendly nod. I want to stop at every lit studio space and just drink in all this wonderful art, but Grayson keeps me to a steady pace, heading for the far corner.

And then we get to Henry's space. It's dominated by enormous acrylic psychedelic paintings—most of them at least twice my height. They remind me of Peter Max's pop art and the sorts of images that you'll find on album covers by West Coast bands, or to advertise a be-in or a love-in. On the easel is a bewilderingly complex mandala that he's rendering in oil. The complimentary colours have been placed just right so that the whole painting seems to vibrate. On a long table is a scatter of life drawings that make me ache with the beauty of their expressive lines. But there's no Henry.

"That's odd," Jeremy says. "He's here *every* night."

I let go of Grayson's arm to take a closer look at the life drawings. I can feel a twitch in my fingers—just like Geordie says he gets when he sees a really good fiddler playing. You know you're not there yet. Maybe you'll never be that good. But all you want to do is go home and practice, practice, practice. That's what these quick charcoal studies of Henry's wake in me. There's so much expression in every fluid line. I expect the figures to leap off the page and dance around the studio.

"You came!" a familiar voice calls out.

It takes me a moment to remember where I am. I turn to see Henry standing behind my intrepid guides, beaming with pleasure.

"I did," I tell him. "And I'm glad I did. Your work's beyond lovely."

"Beyond lovely," Jeremy repeats and winks at Grayson.

Henry's smile broadens.

"Out of here," he says, waving them out of his studio space. "The both of you. I swear," he adds to me, "if they didn't spend so much time pretending to be nineteenth century dandies, they'd actually be pretty decent artists."

"We'd be insulted," Grayson says.

Jeremy nods. "Except sadly, it's true."

"Out," Henry says.

"Thanks for showing me around," I tell them.

"Oh, phish," Jeremy says. "It was nothing."

Grayson lifts a languid hand in my direction and then the pair of them amble off and I'm left alone with Henry. I feel a little shy with them gone, so I turn my attention back to the life studies on the worktable.

"I did those at the ballet studio next door," Henry says.

"It was nice of them to pose for you."

He laughs. "They didn't pose. I just sketched while they practiced their warm-up routines. You should come some time. It's really invigorating and totally loosens up your drawing arm."

"I think mine would fall off."

"The only limitations are those we put on ourselves."

"Yes, well, that's very Zen of you," I tell him, "but I'm nowhere near the skill level needed to produce anything even close to these."

He nods to show that he's heard me, then he says, "The only limitations…"

I laugh. "Are those we put on ourselves. I got it."

"So are you thinking of taking a space here?" he asks.

"I think so. I'd like to."

I'm about to add that it depended on the rent, but then I remember the balance of my bank account this afternoon and realize that the rent would have to be really steep for me to not be able to afford it.

"That's great," he says. He gives me a considering look, then adds, "There's something different about you this evening. It's like you're more here, if that makes any sense."

"Not really," I say. "Nothing has made much sense since I got here a couple of nights ago."

"Oh, you're newly arrived? That explains it. It takes a little while to settle in here—to be really grounded."

As soon as he says that, it occurs to me that, back in my world, Henry's must be dead. I want to ask how he died, but I'm not sure of the protocol. Is that what you do, the way you'd ask a fellow student their major? Or do you wait for them to offer it up when they're ready?

"So have you always been an artist?" I ask instead.

He laughs. I like his laugh. When he laughs, or even smiles, his whole face lights up.

"Hardly," he says. "Before I died, I was pretty much a waste of space. I was always stoned—no hard drugs, but if you smoke up 24-7, it's not like you're going to do much more than lie around and veg, you know? My life just went by in a smoky haze. But then, when I got here…well, it was a revelation. I looked back and saw all that time I'd wasted—the things I could have done, the friendships I could have maintained—and I figured if God or whatever was going to give me a second chance, I wasn't going to screw it up this time."

"So you became an artist."

"I'm trying," he says. "I've got a long way to go."

I look pointedly around the studio.

"Don't kid yourself," he says. "The more you do, the harder it gets. Every time I start a new painting, I almost feel like I have to learn how to do it all over again, because every one's different. Or it should be."

He points to one of the psychedelic canvases. It sort of looks like Jimi Hendrix with his hair turning into this amazing sunburst that explodes out in a swirl of colour to every corner.

"So," he goes on, "I almost figured out how to capture the picture that comes into my head when I listen to Hendrix, but how does that prepare me for this?"

Now he points to the painting of the mandala that's on the easel.

I nod. "But if you work at it regularly, you must develop a certain set of skills that makes it easier to put the pictures in your head down on canvas. You're not struggling with the medium as well."

He smiles. "How long have you been painting?"

"For real? A few months. But I've been drawing all my life."

"Well, you know how you can fight with the paint, or your ground, or just the damn light as it shifts?"

I nod.

"That never goes away," he says. "Sure, I know if I mix these colours, I'll get that tone. I know the theories of composition and perspective, how to use my negative space, all that stuff. But getting what I see in my head down on the paper or canvas? It's still a challenge. Every time."

I smile. "Well, that's really encouraging."

"Think how boring it would be if it was any different. You'd just be like a factory, spitting out product. And you *can* paint that way. I just don't think of it as art."

"Because it has to mean something."

"Exact-a-mundo."

I lift my eyebrows. I don't think I've ever heard someone say that with a straight face.

"Anyway," he says, "the point is, I was a loser before I died, and if I didn't want the same thing to happen to me here, I had to reinvent myself. I had to become the guy I could have been back when. Hell, should have been." He smiles and shrugs. "I don't know. Does that make any sense?"

"Unfortunately," I tell him, "it makes all too much sense."

"Because you've been there."

I nod. I know all about reinventing yourself.

–6–

Police officer Lou Fucceri found me in the doorway of a Palm Street shop when I was pretty much as far down as you can go without actually being dead. I hadn't eaten in days. I hadn't had a fix in almost as long. I was this dirty, strung-out junkie—about as appealing as some scraggly stray cat, or a feral dog, so it wasn't like I had any hope of attracting a john. Not even for a blowjob. But Lou saw something in me. When he asked me my name, I made one up on the spot.

I didn't know it at the time, but I buried Jillian Carter that day.

Lou took me to the office of his girlfriend, a woman named Angelina Marceau. People called her Angel—the Grasso Street Angel—because she had this streetfront counseling service on Grasso Street. She'd help anybody, but she specialized in street kids and runaways.

It was a couple of hours past midnight when we got there, but she was still in her office, sitting behind a big desk, a mass of paperwork spread out in front of her. She looked a little tired, but she was still gorgeous: tall, with a heart-shaped face and a long, dark waterfall of auburn hair that seemed to go forever down her back. She smiled when she saw Lou, her eyes going sad when they reached me.

There was compassion in those eyes, not pity, but I still felt small and dirty, standing there in my filthy clothes and greasy hair. I ducked my head and stared at the floor.

There wasn't much in the room. Besides her desk, there was a rack of filing cabinets along one wall, an old beat-up sofa with a matching chair by the bay window, a pair of oak straightbacks on the other side of the room by the desk. I eyed the sofa, but knew if I sat down on it, I'd never get back up again. I noticed a small table beside the filing cabinets with a kettle on a hot plate. Beside it was a coffee maker and a bowl of tea bags, sugar and hot chocolate packets.

"This is Jilly," Lou said. "I don't know if she'll stay, but I thought I'd bring her by to at least hear what you have to say."

Angel nodded. "Why don't you give us some time alone."

"Sure. I'm still on duty. If you need to reach me—"

"I can call you through dispatch," she finished.

Lou touched my shoulder—a feather-soft brush of his fingers.

"You take care," he said.

I didn't answer. What was I supposed to say? I was long past taking care of anything.

"Do you need anything, Jilly?" Angel asked when the door closed behind Lou and we were alone in her office.

Her voice was like her eyes, warm and compassionate. I stared at the floor for a moment longer, then looked up to meet her gaze.

"Yeah," I said. "Have you got a fix?"

The corner of her mouth twitched.

"I was thinking more of something to drink," she said. "Tea, maybe, or a coffee. Something to eat. Maybe you'd like to take a shower."

I shuffled over to one of the straightbacks and sat down. I raised my feet to the edge of the seat so that I could hug my knees. It helped stop the shakes.

"All of the above," I said. "But mostly a fix."

"We'll get to that."

"So your boyfriend the cop...he said I wasn't busted."

"That's right. I have no official status with any government agency, on any level. You can walk out of here any time you want."

"Then maybe I just will."

She nodded. "It's your choice."

I didn't move. If I held onto my knees, really tightly, all the trembling only seemed to happen on the inside. Did I want to walk out? It was warm in here. And dry. It smelled good, too. The coffee maker must have finished brewing a new pot just before the cop brought me in.

"Lou says you're an artist," she said.

I snorted. "Yeah, right."

"But you're carrying some of your art in your knapsack, aren't you?"

"If you want to call it that. It's nothing. Just crap."

"Then why do you carry it around?" she asked.

I didn't really have an answer for her. I knew why I drew—I'd always drawn. It was something that took me out of myself, but at the same time, it took me deeper into myself in a way that I could deal with what I found there. But I wasn't about to tell her that.

"Look, could we just get to the point?" I said.

"The point?"

"You know. The lecture, or the religious come-on, or whatever the hell it is that you're selling here."

"There's no lecture and I'm not recruiting for any religion or cult."

"Then what the hell is this place?"

She gave me a long, considering look, then she told me. How she helped kids get off the street by finding them sponsors, people who'd pay for lodgings while they finished school, or who'd help them find a job, or even co-sign a student loan.

"What's stops you all from getting ripped off?"

"My judgment," she said.

"You're that good at getting a fix on people?"

She shrugged.

"And what do the Good Samaritans get out of the deal? A little nookie on the side?"

"The pleasure of helping people who just need somebody to care about them to make a better life for themselves."

"Yeah, like that's going to happen."

"We've got a pretty good track record so far."

I cocked my head. "You're serious."

"Of course I'm serious."

"So you…what? Look at me and decide you're going to help me and I'm not going to fuck it up, or rip you off?"

"Actually, I haven't decided yet."

"Oh."

"I need you to be clean first."

I gave her a slow shake of my head.

"I don't see that happening," I told her. "It's not like I haven't… you know…"

"Tried already."

I nodded.

"If you want to, and you're serious about it," she said, "I'll make sure you get through it in one piece."

"Just like that."

"Oh, I'm not saying it'll be pretty or easy. But at least you'll have somebody in your corner who gives a damn."

I wanted to call her on that—why the hell should she care?—but there was this thing about her…the calmness, the look in her eyes, the whole vibe.

"Why me?" I asked. "Why me and not somebody else?"

She smiled. "Because right now, you're the one sitting here in front of me."

Angel was right. It was neither pretty, nor easy. But just as she promised, she also stayed with me through it all. Through the chills and the fevers. Through me screaming at her and calling her every foul name I ever used on my brother. Through me trying to hit her—actually I think I landed a few because later, when I could finally pay attention to something other than my own pain, I saw she had a black eye.

I felt horrible about it, but then I felt horrible about everything. Being clean didn't seem to help much. The physical being clean, I mean. I don't know that it ever goes away inside your head.

I was so weak when Angel took me out of the detox place and got me a room in the Chelsea Arms that she pretty much had to carry me to the cab, and then up to my room. Then I spent forever crying, and aching. Everything felt wrong. I was a stranger inside this weird emaciated body that carried me from the bed, to the toilet, then back to the bed. I ached constantly—mostly inside. My eyes were almost swollen shut from crying.

Angel told me to order food from room service, but I never ate until she came by to see me and brought me some soup or tea. I stayed in the bed until Angel dragged me into the shower. Then she wouldn't let me go back to bed until a chambermaid had come in and changed the sheets.

I had no idea how long I went through this until one day I was actually sitting in a chair, staring out the window, when Angel came in. I'd had a shower on my own, but I only wore one of a half dozen oversized T-shirts that Angel had left in the room when I first checked in.

"Well, this is new," Angel said.

I shrugged. Her bruising was reduced to some yellowy-green discolouration around her eye, but I still felt bad about it every time I saw her.

"Are you feeling any better?" Angel went on as if we were going to actually have a conversation.

She put a take-out container of noodle soup on the table beside my chair.

"Define better," I said.

"As in you don't feel like either lying in bed all day, or killing yourself." She paused, then added, "Or anybody else."

She didn't raise her hand to her bruised eye, but she didn't have to.

"I'm so sorry—" I began.

She cut me off with a wave of her hand. "I know. I wasn't talking about my eye. That was just an accident. I meant all those people you were ranting about. Someone named Del. Someone else named Rob. A priest..."

"My brother, my loser boyfriend, and the parish priest with a yen for little girls. Maybe little boys, too. I don't know."

Angel nodded through my explanation, but made no comment, though I did see her eyes tighten.

"No," I went on. "I don't want to kill anybody anymore. Though if any of them was to get run over by some big huge truck, I wouldn't be shedding any tears."

She studied me for a long moment, then finally nodded again.

"What?" I said.

She smiled. "What do you want to do now?"

"Just like that, I'm cured?"

She shook her head. "We both know it doesn't work like that. To be honest, I don't know if you'll ever stop wanting a fix. There's a reason why people who've been clean for years still refer to themselves as junkies."

I nodded.

"And the things you had to go through as a kid and on the street…"

"They're not going to go away either."

"Not any time soon," she said.

"So when you asked what did I want to do…"

"Everybody's different," she said. "But in my experience, the best way to try to put those sorts of things behind you is to make a new life for yourself. Immerse yourself in it so that you're too busy to sit around and brood."

"That works?"

"It helps. And at least you'll be doing something for yourself."

I gave a slow nod.

"So let me repeat the question," she said. "What do you want to do now? Who do you want to be?"

Who did I want to be? Anybody but Jillian Carter. When I looked in a mirror using her name, I saw only a victim. A loser. Poor white trash from Hillbilly Holler—which is what the townies called the part of Tyson where I grew up.

"I…I don't have any I.D.," I said.

"We can get copies of your birth certificate and—did you ever get your Social Insurance Number?"

I shook my head. "But I don't want to be…*her*. I need to be somebody new. I need to be Jilly Coppercorn with no ties to that old life of mine. I don't want a legal name change. I need to *be* somebody else without a paper that says I changed my name from this to that."

Angel didn't say anything for a long moment.

"We can do that, too," she said finally. "But it has to stay between us. Lou can't ever know. Nobody can."

"You can do that?" I repeated. "You'd do that for me?"

Because I could tell it was a big deal.

She nodded. "I'll get a…friend started on the paperwork."

"I don't know what to say."

"You don't have to say anything. And now…"

"I want to go to art school," I said. "I want to be like a normal person and go to university and everything,"

She studied me again. "You look young enough. We can adjust your age on the new I.D. if you like."

I shook my head. "I don't need to pretend to be younger. I just want a chance at a normal life."

"Okay. We can do that. I can hook you up with an accelerated high school program over the winter. If you work hard, I think we can get you into Butler U. for the first semester next fall." She paused for a moment, then added, "You know while we're getting this other paperwork, I could probably get you a high school diploma while I'm at it."

"Are you serious?"

She nodded.

I didn't really have to think about it.

"No," I told her. "I want to actually learn this stuff."

"I'm glad to hear that. I'll get working on that new I.D. for you."

I smiled. "So I guess you decided."

"Decided what?"

"To trust me."

She matched my smile and shook her head. "No, Jilly. *You* decided. I'm just along for the ride."

Staying clean wasn't easy. It helped that I had all the schoolwork. I also had Angel's support, and the support of Lou and the ragtag bunch of people who hung out in her streetfront office. But through that first autumn, mostly it was Angel.

Maybe I was like a baby duck and had imprinted on her or something, but once I got clean—when the brown wasn't my Bible and sacrament anymore—the only time I felt normal was when I was around her. Or even just being in her office, which felt like being with her even when she wasn't there. I'd sit and do my homework. When that was done, I'd read ahead in my school books, or sketch. I helped out around the office, too. Making coffee, sweeping up, keeping the files in order, running errands, answering the phone.

One of the regulars at the office—I can't remember who, but I think it was Denny. He used to be a wino; now he does odd jobs up and down the block. He echoed what Angel had told me before, saying that the best way to fight the jones was to make a clean break with your past. "Don't hang around with your old crowd," he told me. "Don't go to your old hangouts. Maybe in a few years you can, but right now all it's going to do is drag you right back into that life. It's easy to be righteous going to school, or sitting here in Angel's office. But what if you're in a bar and some old friend wants to buy you a beer? You run into your dealer and he offers to fix you up for free— you know, for old time's sake? You're sitting around, shooting the bull, and suddenly the joint that's been making the rounds is sitting there, right in your fingers."

He was right, but it was easier for me than maybe he thought it would be. That's because I didn't really have any friends back then. Just guys who used me. People I shared needles and squats with. There was Donna, but if she was still strung out, all she was going to do was suck me back into that life.

Later, I thought. Later I'll track her down and introduce her to Angel. To what life can be like when you don't have to see it through a haze of booze and dope. But I couldn't risk it now.

I had an allowance from whomever my sponsor was—he or she wanted to remain anonymous, so I could only thank Angel. But I knew if I was going on to university after I graduated high school, I was going to need more money than that. I got a couple of crappy jobs—behind the counter at a fast food joint, cashier at the local grocery store—but then I totally lucked out. A friend of Angel's pulled a few strings and got me on at the Post Office, and just like that, my life changed again.

It wasn't just that the money and hours were better—and they were, for sure. No, it was there that I made my first real friend since

Donna had befriended me in the Home for Wayward Girls all those years ago. I thought of Angel and Lou and Denny and some of the others as friends, of course, but it wasn't the same. They were either helping me, or people I met through Angel and Lou.

Of course, I didn't know that when I first met Geordie Riddell—that we would connect the way we did, I mean. We bumped into each other in the doorway of the cafeteria—literally—two scruffs, the one of us shyer than the other, which is odd when you consider how we turned out. Geordie's full of life and jokes—especially when he's busking or on stage—while I've become "relentlessly cheerful," as one of the bag boys at the grocery store said a week or so before I quit. He meant it negatively, but I took it as a compliment.

We all want the world to be a better place. Where better to start than with yourself? It was hard at first, but I grew to love smiling and chatting with just about anybody. The smile I got in return was all the reward I needed.

But it all started with Geordie. He was the first friend I made on my own. He drew me out of my shell—I guess he was so good at it, because he had a wall of his own that he lived behind. We didn't share war stories, but they were sitting there in our eyes and our pasts, and I guess just the fact that they were there helped us connect with each other. And we were just friends.

It wasn't that he was homely or anything. He and his brother Christy—whom I met later—are a handsome pair of lads. But I needed a friend, not a lover. I'd shared my body with too many people where it meant nothing.

Mind you, I couldn't spend a lot of time with Geordie. I had two jobs—I'd started on as a waitress at a diner as well as working at the Post Office. I had school. And I thought it was important to continue to make myself useful around Angel's office. So mostly, in those early days as autumn froze into winter, Geordie and I just shared our lunch breaks at work.

I told him a little bit about Angel's work. I didn't lie about how I'd ended up there, I just didn't dwell on it. Most of the time I was still a mess anyway. I could keep it together at work and school, but when I was alone in my room at the Chelsea Arms, or walking down the streets going to or from work and Angel's place, I could sometimes feel myself just…unraveling. If I looked behind me, I was sure I'd see the sidewalk littered with bits and pieces of myself that had just fallen away.

"It's never going to be easy," Angel said when I brought it up one day. "Especially not when you're in your own head with no distractions."

"I'll be cool," I told her.

The last thing I needed was for Angel or my sponsor to get cold feet and cut me off from this one chance of being somebody I wanted to be, instead of the waste of space I'd been.

"You need to keep your mind busy," Angel said. "Here's what I do when I need a distraction. I look at the people going by and I make up stories about them."

I couldn't imagine Angel needing to be distracted from anything, but it was good advice and after I'd tried it a few times, I tucked it away in my little mental satchel of things that helped.

It's funny. I totally appreciated Angel and these anonymous sponsors of hers, but I still didn't get *why* they did what they did. I mean, I understood the concept of charity work, and it wasn't like I was completely heartless. If I saw some old bag lady on the street, sure, I'd feel sorry for her and everything. Maybe if she spilled her cart, I'd help her get it upright again and put her junk back in. Maybe scare off a kid if he was bugging her.

But I didn't want to make a project out of her—do you know what I mean? I wasn't out to save her or anything.

I couldn't even save myself.

But Angel was just there for anybody who needed her help. She was always talking some kid down from a bad trip, or the junkie shakes. She'd be negotiating with police and social services to keep another one out of juvie or a foster home. She'd be bailing someone out, or visiting someone in the hospital. I really understood why people called her the Grasso Street Angel because she wasn't ready to give up on anybody.

But the people she was helping weren't always so grateful.

Sometimes, when I'd be doing my homework in the main room, she or her client wouldn't close the door to the inner office and I could hear everything they were saying.

I'd been a perfect little shit the first time I met her, but my strung-out bad temper seemed positively benign compared to the way some of these kids treated her. A doormat outside the worst dive on Palm Street got more respect.

I'd sit there, getting madder and madder, until all I wanted to do was go in and whack whichever mouthy kid it was up the side of his or her head. But it didn't seem to faze Angel in the least. Her patience and...just her calmness blew me away.

"How do you do it?" I asked after one particularly nasty kid tore a strip off Angel, then stomped out of the office, slamming the door behind her.

"Do what?" she asked.

"Stay so calm when they treat you like that."

She shrugged. "Sometimes they need to vent and I don't mind being their verbal punching bag. Not if it means that I might get the chance to help them."

"I don't know. It still seems fu—uh, messed up."

I've been trying to clean up my language, but it's hard. If I don't think about it, I slip right back.

Angel nodded. "It is messed up. But if these kids *weren't* messed up, they wouldn't be needing my help, would they?"

"I guess. But it's not something I could ever do."

"You might surprise yourself," she said. "Not that I'm pushing for you to become a social worker—I think you have another path ahead of you. But I don't want you to sell yourself short."

"I won't. Or at least I'll try not to. But sometimes, it all seems so..."

"Overwhelming?"

I nodded. "And hard."

"You're doing really well," she said. "I'm proud of you."

I just looked at her. People had said a lot of things to me in the past, but I couldn't remember anyone ever telling me that.

Making friends with Geordie was a big change in my life. Another came one night in late spring. Angel was out—I can't remember where—and I was in the office doing my homework when the front door burst open and this kid came stumbling in. She looked a worse mess that I had been at my lowest—just this skinny kid with long stringy hair, pasty skin, and those haunted, dark-rimmed eyes that held her jones deep in each hollow. Shoeless, in torn fishnet stockings, wearing a jean miniskirt and a tight tube top, she looked like she'd been lying in the mud somewhere. I couldn't tell how old she was—she could have been anywhere from her teens to her late twenties.

She stood in the doorway for a long moment, hugging herself to stop from shaking. Her gaze skittered around the room until it finally settled on me.

"Where—where's Angel?" she demanded.

"She had to go out. Can I—"

"Fuck you. I can't take this shit anymore."

"Look I—"

"They took my baby!"

"Who did?"

I was thinking, dealers, some other crack whore.

"Fucking social services!" she yelled. "They just fucking took her!"

And maybe for good reason, I thought, all things considered. But I wasn't going there right now. I just wanted to settle her down.

I stood up from the desk where I'd been studying.

"Come sit on the sofa," I said. "I'll get you a coffee."

"I don't want your fucking coffee. I want my baby. Where's Angel? She said she'd help me. She's supposed to fucking *be* here!"

"She had to go out. She'll be back soon."

"Soon, soon. What the fuck does that mean?"

"Just soon," I repeated.

I tried to keep my voice soothing, though I was starting to lose my patience. I knew she was strung out—I'd been there, and it's not pretty—but I still wanted to just give her a good slap and tell her to stop being so self-absorbed. If she wanted things to change, she had to change them herself. Nobody else could do it for her, and being rude to those who might try to help her didn't do any good.

But then I'd needed help with that first big step, hadn't I? And this wasn't my world, it was Angel's—where everybody deserved a second chance.

I went over to where she was standing and tried to steer her to the sofa in the inner office. She pulled away when I put my hand on her arm, but she let herself be herded through the door. When she sat on the couch, she slumped as though all the bones in her body had turned to jelly—though that didn't stop the shakes.

She sat up and hugged herself again, bent over, staring at the floor. I hoped she wasn't going to throw up. I really didn't feel like cleaning it up.

"Fuck it," she said in a small voice. "I should just let them keep her—she'll be better off."

I sat down beside her, but I didn't say anything. What was I going to say? Yeah, I agree?

That dark-rimmed hollow gaze of hers turned to me.

"Angel will figure something out," I said.

I didn't know that she would—that she even could—but I felt I had to say something. The girl's gaze was still too jittery and she couldn't quite focus on mine.

"What's your name?" I asked.

"Just call me Skeeter—that's what everybody does."

"Okay, Skeeter it is. My name's Jilly."

She nodded, like she was happy to be sharing. But then she made it clear what she really needed.

"You got any dope here?" she asked. "Anything, man. Even some uppers—just to see me through."

"No. Sorry."

She turned away.

"Of course you fucking don't," she said, and went back to staring at the floor.

I looked for something else to say and really, *really* wished Angel would get back.

"Christ, I've really messed it up this time," Skeeter said suddenly. "They're never going to give her back to me."

"You don't know that."

"The fuck I don't. But she'll be better off with them. I'm such a fucking waste of space—what can I give her? I should just kill myself and get it over with."

She fell silent and the silence stretched between us, long and uncomfortable. I started to panic. What if she was serious?

I stole a glance to the doorway. Where was Angel?

"You can't do that," I finally said.

"What, kill myself?"

I nodded.

"Why not?"

"Nothing's that bad," I said.

"How the fuck would you know?"

So I told her the story of my life so far.

She wasn't a good listener. She kept interrupting and making comments, but it turned out the way we'd grown up wasn't dissimilar. It had been her uncle, not her brother. A teacher in high school, not a priest. But we'd both ended up in juvie and foster homes and eventually the streets. Like me, she'd turned to drugs to see herself through the dark, then prostitution to pay for the drugs, though her pimp got most of the money. I knew that story too well.

The only big difference was, I'd never had a kid.

"I thought Allison would change everything," Skeeter said. "And she did, but not in a good way. Johnny—" That was her pimp. "—didn't want anything to do with her. Allison didn't turn us into a family. She tore us apart."

"Johnny should have been the least of your worries."

"He wasn't that bad—most of the time."

"Yeah, I'll bet he was real nice when he wasn't pimping your ass to put some cash in his own pocket."

Anger flared in her eyes. "What the fuck do you know?" she said, then caught herself and nodded. "Yeah, I guess you do."

"Been there—done that," I said.

She nodded again. "What am I going to do?"

"I have no idea. But Angel will. She can help you. I mean if she can help me, she can help anybody."

"I guess." There was a long pause before she asked, "Was it hard? Getting clean?"

"Hardest thing I ever did."

"But it's good now? You're good?"

"I won't lie to you," I told her. "Like Angel says, there's a good reason that people who've been clean for twenty years still refer to themselves as addicts. I'm just hoping it'll get easier."

She shook her head. "Then what's the point?"

"I'm guessing it'll be different for everybody. For me, I..." I stopped a moment to think it through. "I guess it was that all my life I've been shaped by what other people thought of me, and until I met Angel and Lou, nobody thought very much of me at all. There was my friend Donna from juvie, but she was as messed up as me, so I don't know if that really counts. All I know for sure is, I don't like being the person my family, or my pimp, or most of straight society convinced me I was. I just...I just got tired of being the victim, I guess."

"But now you're not."

I shrugged. "I don't know exactly who I am right now. Somebody in transition, I guess. Somebody who was royally fucked up who's now trying to be less fucked up—at least about the stuff I can control. I can't control the way other people are going to see me. All I can do is give them different clues. If I don't look like a strung-out hooker, then maybe they won't see me that way anymore."

"Why do you care what other people think?" Skeeter asked.

"Mostly, I don't. But I have to live in the same world as everybody else and I'd rather have the chance to say my piece instead of getting dismissed out of hand because of the way I look."

"So you're going to go completely straight."

I laughed. "Does this look straight?"

I looked pretty much the way I always did these days: not quite so skin-and-bones anymore, but I was still thin, and definitely scruffy. Wearing the baggy clothes I did, and with the way my hair was forever in a wild tangle, I didn't fit anybody's image of clean-cut.

"So, no," I said. "I'm not going completely straight—unless you're talking about dope-free. But when people see me, the first thing they're going to think isn't that I'm strung-out."

"I wish I could just..." Skeeter began.

But then we heard the front door open and she fell silent. A moment later, Angel was in the office and Skeeter was telling her about her daughter.

"We really need to get her back," Skeeter said, finishing up.

"Oh, Kelly—I'm sorry. I mean Skeeter. But do you really think that's such a good idea?"

I saw the anger flood her face, but then she caught herself the way she had earlier when she and I were talking.

"I can't leave her with them," she said. Her voice was tight, but with worry and pain, and—I could tell—the need for a hit. "She can't go through the crap I did."

Angel was sitting across from us, on the edge of her desk. I watched her lips purse as she thought.

"Are you still getting along with your grandmother?" she finally asked.

Skeeter nodded.

"And you trust her?"

"Yeah, she's the only one who never screwed me over and Christ knows I gave her reason."

"Okay, we'll see if we can get Allison released into your grandmother's custody. But before we do anything, you need a shower and a change of clothes."

Skeeter gave another nod and Angel's eyebrow went up.

"What?" Angel said. "You're not going to ask for enough to score just a little hit first?"

Skeeter looked at me, before she turned back to Angel.

"No," she said. "Once we make sure Allison's safe with Grandma, I'd like to...you know..."

Angel didn't make it easy for her, but I guess this wasn't something you could do for a person. They had to make the decision for themselves because they were the only ones who could hold themselves to it.

"I need your help, Angel," she said. "I really need to fix my life."

Angel nodded and scooted off the desk. "Okay. Let's see about that shower."

Skeeter and I stood up from the sofa.

"So your real name's Kelly?" I asked.

She nodded. "People just called me Skeeter because I'm small and, you know, busy. Like a mosquito"

"My real name's Jillian."

She shook my hand, but then she didn't let it go.

"I...I think maybe you just saved my life," she said. "Me and Allison, both."

"I didn't do anything."

"Yeah, you did. I thought I'd hit the bottom before, but today...today there was no bottom. Today there was just this black empty space and I was falling through it. I was swallowed up by it."

"I've been there," I told her.

"I know. You told me. And that was like...I don't know...like a way out, you know? It told me that maybe there was a way out...even for someone like me...and I just..."

She let go of my hand, but it was only to give me a hug. I stiffened for a moment—I still had personal space issues—but then I put my arms around her and hugged her back. I met Angel's gaze over Skeeter's shoulder. She had a considering look in her eyes, but she didn't say anything when Skeeter and I stepped apart except to ask me to lock up when I went back to the hotel. Then the two of them left.

I stood for a long moment in the empty office before I returned to the other room and went back to my homework.

Angel came by my room at the Chelsea Arms later that evening to tell me how things had gone. They'd managed to have Skeeter's daughter released into her Grandmother's care on the condition that Skeeter checked into a detox center. Angel had just left her there.

"You did good today," Angel said.

I shrugged. "I didn't do anything, really."

"No, I think Kelly was right. You did save her life. She's come close to killing herself before and the only thing that would stop her was worrying about what would happen to her daughter. But once they took Allison away…"

"I'm glad I never made that mistake—you know, having a kid."

"It's not always a mistake. Sometimes it's the one thing that turns everything around."

"I suppose."

"What made you think to share your past with her today?"

"Honestly, I didn't know what else to do. I just got scared when she started talking about killing herself and how I wouldn't understand. I wanted her to know that I did. Or at least that I'd been where she'd been. I was just never brave enough to seriously consider killing myself."

"That's not bravery," Angel said. "That's the final pit of hopelessness and despair."

"Then I never hit the real bottom, I guess."

Angel shook her head. "It's different for everybody." She studied me for a moment, before she went on. "I never really thought about how powerful the sharing of a story like yours can be. I was wondering if you'd consider recording it for us. I promise you, it would only be used in cases like Kelly's and we would keep it anonymous."

"I don't know…" Then I sighed. "Do you really think it would help?"

"It helped Kelly. And I'm sure it would help others."

"But to make a recording of it…"

"Would you rather tell that story over and over again?"

I shook my head. I'd already thought I'd been done with it before I sat down with Skeeter in Angel's office.

"I guess one more time wouldn't hurt," I said.

It wasn't easy making that recording. I felt embarrassed and awkward the whole time, the words thick in my mouth. The only way I could do it was to pretend I was telling it to Skeeter again, but even then I first had to get Geordie to help me drag the big reel-to-reel recorder over to the hotel and then sit there in the dark by myself to make it work.

I sat there for a long time after I was done and turned the machine off. When I finally went to bed, I thought I knew what I wanted to do with my life.

"I want to do this," I told Angel after Geordie and I had brought the recorder back to the office and he'd gone off to rehearse with some guys he was playing with this weekend. "What you do. I want to help people."

She nodded. "That's great, Jilly. Really."

I could hear the unspoken "but" without her needing to say it.

"But you don't trust me not to screw it up," I said for her.

"No, no, no. It's not that. I just think you should finish school first."

"My exams are in a month. Once they're over…"

My voice trailed off as she continued to shake her head.

"I meant art school," she said. "You need to explore that avenue. It's so much a part of you."

That's what I got for telling her about this dream I'd always had of making art for a living. Weren't people allowed to change their dreams?

But she was right. If I was honest with myself, I didn't have the dedication to put into the years of schooling it would take to be a social worker. Not because I wasn't capable of doing it—I think I was starting to get it now that maybe I really could do whatever I put my mind to—but because at the end of the day, I didn't care about all the peripheral stuff. I just wanted to help people.

I could do the intensive study thing with art because everything about it interested me—the doing, the viewing, the history, *every-thing*. But helping people…it just seemed so basic. You listened to them. You found out what they needed. Then you tried to help them achieve it. You didn't need a diploma for that.

"I suppose you're right," I said.

Angel smiled. "But there are other things you can do *while* you're going to university."

And she was right. It made my life a bit more complicated, but I discovered that if you want to—if you *make* the effort—you can fit an awful lot into one day. So in between school, working part-time at the Post Office and my shifts at the diner, I started volunteering at the local soup kitchen and St. Vincent's Home for the Aged. Once a week I joined the old ladies at St. Paul's and helped them go through the donations they received for their monthly rummage sale. I wasn't a practicing Catholic anymore—I didn't even know if I'd call myself a Christian these days—but I liked the ladies and the money they raised helped the less fortunate in the neighbourhood, and that seemed like a good thing no matter what religious persuasion you might happen to follow.

I wasn't saving lives. And I wasn't making that big a difference in the overall scheme of things. But you know what? It didn't matter. I was doing good on a small scale and it helped me connect with people in a way I never had before. I used to be scared of everyone I met because I didn't know what they were going to do to me. Okay, I have to admit, I hadn't quite gotten over that yet. But I discovered there were a lot of good people in the world. Some of them were down on their luck. Some of them—like the folks in St. Vincent's—didn't have anybody except for the caregivers. No family. No friends. It was often hard for them to just get around their room, never mind going out somewhere.

Not everybody was wonderful, but most of them were, and the ones who weren't had pretty good reasons for being cranky or nervous or unhappy. They all—the good and the bad—taught me to think beyond my own little world. They taught me to relate to people as people. They taught me to be cheerful and to smile.

It's funny how much good a real smile does. It breaks down age barriers, cultural barriers, any kind of barrier.

So I was busy, busy, busy, but I didn't mind. And you know what? When you're worrying over other people's problems you don't have nearly so much time to focus on your own.

And then, just when I'd settled into a comfortable routine, it was time to start my first year at Butler University.

I really did want to go to university—it was something that no one in my family had ever done. If you talked to a Carter about such a thing, they'd think it was a hoot. You might as well just throw your money away. I don't know that anyone in my family even finished high school like I just had.

But I was different from them. I liked to learn. The high school course just confirmed that for me. And I *loved* to draw. The idea that I could go somewhere and for three or four years, do both seemed like unbelievable bliss. I was out of the hotel now and living in my own place in a rooming house close to campus. Life seemed perfect.

But the reality wasn't, because part of attending university was interacting with other people—meeting other people. *Lots* of other people. People who didn't need or want anything from me. They weren't the wino at the soup kitchen who seemed to appreciate a smile and a kind word as much as the meal. They weren't the old lady at St. Vincent's who was so happy to find someone who'd listen to all her stories about growing up in Lower Foxville, back before it got all run-down and worn out. They weren't the kid at Angel's office who just wanted to sit with someone who didn't expect anything from her and would keep her safe. Or the old ladies at St. Paul's, grateful to have an extra hand sorting through donations.

I found it totally overwhelming.

None of the kids wanted anything much to do with me. I don't think it was because I was a couple of years older than them—with my small size I actually looked younger than a lot of them, or at least the same age. I just wasn't particularly cool or interesting, I guess. And I suppose a lot of it was my fault. For all that I'd been learning to be more extroverted in the rest of my life, at university I just fell back into the bad habit of shrinking into my own skin.

I *wanted* to be outgoing and meet people, but they scared me, too. The old folks and street people didn't ask a lot of personal questions. They'd listen, if you wanted to tell them, but they didn't push. The university kids were different—it was like they had no concept of personal space. You'd meet someone and they'd just start firing questions at you, a lot of which I couldn't answer because I didn't want them to see me as that kind of person.

Maybe I'm being unfair. Maybe I just met the wrong people out of the gate. Whatever it was, I ended up wandering through campus and attending my classes like a ghost. I didn't want to be noticed and I guess I got good at it because I as much as disappeared into the woodwork so far as the profs and other students were concerned.

I started to get a kind of agoraphobia. Is there one for where you're okay unless you're in one particular place? Which in my case, would be the Butler U. campus. Whatever, three weeks into my classes I found myself unable to walk through the door of that afternoon's life drawing. I stopped at the door, then backed into the hallway again.

I knew the panic rising up in me was stupid. I knew I should just walk in and take my place at a free easel. But I couldn't. I dropped my army surplus backpack on the floor, then sat down beside it and hugged my knees. A few people walked by, going into the class. I didn't look at them, but I could tell they were looking at me. I hoped they were just curious. I hoped that what I was feeling wasn't written all over my face for the whole world to laugh at.

Then one set of legs stopped in front of me.

Nice shoes, I thought. Clunky like Doc Martin's, but not the black I'd always seen them in. These were an oak brown, with pink socks above them and black cotton trouser legs above *them*.

"Are you okay?" the voice belonging to the nice shoes asked.

I slowly lifted my gaze.

She was about my size, but with more wattage than I could ever hope to muster: way prettier, with thick gorgeous hair and real curves as opposed to my more boyish figure. I didn't know her name, but I'd seen her in class. She was always smiling when our gazes met, but I was too shy to do much more than duck my head and hide behind my hair. Which I did again now.

"Are you stoned?" she asked when I didn't respond.

I shook my head.

"Then I guess you're having a panic attack."

Surprise lifted my gaze once more and pushed a word out of my throat: "How..?"

"I know the look," she said. "I used to get them all the time after my mother disappeared."

She put her back against the wall and slid down on the floor beside me.

"Your mother disappeared?" I said.

She nodded. "Yeah. I was just a kid when it happened, so I guess that messed me up more than it would have if I'd been older. But I doubt it's ever an easy thing to deal with."

I wouldn't know. There'd been a lot of times I'd have given anything to have my mother disappear.

"She just walked out the door one day and never came back. Of course I thought it was my fault. And I was sure my dad would also desert me, so for the next six months, every time he stepped out of my sight, I'd have this huge freak-out."

"That sounds horrible."

She nodded. "It wasn't fun. I got better about it, but I still have this feeling that anybody I care about is going to just up and disappear on me one day. It's not a matter of maybe, but when." She shook her head and smiled. "God, listen to me. My friend Wendy says the reason I don't make friends easily is because I keep everybody at arm's length, but here I am dumping my whole life story on you."

I kept wanting to drop my gaze back to the floor, but I made myself look at her for a long moment. She was so beautiful. The way the light fell on her hair made her look like an angel, all aglow. I would just love to paint her.

"I don't mind," I told her. "I know, from having a messed up childhood."

I didn't add that I was also an ex-junkie and hooker, but the unspoken words echoed in my head.

She didn't press me to elaborate. Instead, she said, "It's weird how many ordinary-looking people are actually walking around hiding the fact that they're damaged goods." She laughed, but without much humour. "Not that that's the kind of thing you necessarily want to broadcast to the whole wide world on a regular basis."

I nodded. But I had to ask, "So why did you?"

"Tell you?"

I nodded again.

"I don't know. I've been meaning to talk to you anyway—from seeing you in class. You…I don't know how to explain it. You just have this light about you and something about the way it shines in me tells me we could be friends."

I couldn't hide my surprise. She patted my knee and laughed.

"Oh, don't worry," she said. "I like boys. This is something different. And now you must think I'm a complete fruitcake."

It was funny. When she started talking about this light and how we could be friends, I'd realized I'd already started to feel the same way. Not about the light, whatever that meant. But the friends part, for sure. It was like when I met Donna in juvie. I'd been nervous about letting myself care, but when I did allow for the possibility that maybe we could be friends, everything just fell into place.

Maybe that could happen here. I didn't know.

But what I did know was that talking to her had completely eased the tightness in my chest. For the first time on campus I felt the way I did at Angel's office, or on the street. Angel was forever telling me that the best way to overcome nervousness was to get so wrapped up in something so that you forgot to be afraid. It made intellectual sense, but didn't seem to be practical when you were actually in the middle of your anxiety. But it turned out she was right.

"No," I told her. "I'm glad you stopped to talk to me."

"I'm Sophie," she said and offered me her hand. "Sophie Etoile. Apparently that means 'star' in French."

"I'm Jilly Coppercorn," I said as I shook her hand, "and my name just means me, I guess."

She smiled. "So are you staying in the hall for this class?"

I glanced at the doorway and shrugged. "I'd feel stupid going in now. Everybody saw me out here. And besides, what's the point?"

Sophie arched her eyebrows.

"I'm a phony," I explained. "I'm not an artist and I don't know what I'm doing here."

"Don't be silly," she said. "We're none of us artists here."

"Right. Have you seen the work of some of the other students? Have you looked at what's on your own easel?"

She smiled. "So some of us are a little ahead of others, but none of us are what we could be. Not yet. That's what we're here to learn."

"I suppose. At least it sounds good in theory."

"So let's cut class," she said. "It's well past noon. We could go to Kathryn's for a beer."

"I kind of don't do alcohol at the moment," I told her.

She did the question with her eyebrows again.

"I don't really have a problem with it," I explained, "but it puts me in the mood where my other problems are harder to refuse. I...I haven't been clean for very long."

Again she didn't press me.

"Then how about some hot chocolate?" she asked. "Chocolate cures all, you know. It's a proven medical fact."

"It is?"

She shrugged. "Well, if it isn't, it should be."

"Chocolate would be good," I told her.

"Then let's away!"

I got up with her and shot a last guilty look at the classroom door before I followed her outside. I was only here on the sufferance of the sponsors Angel had found for me. Blowing off classes didn't seem like a good way to repay them.

"We can still go back to class," Sophie said.

I shook my head. "No, I need a break."

She grinned. "Or we could always draw each other when we get to Kathryn's."

Kathryn's Café was a college hangout that a lot of the arts students went to, but I'd never been there before. I didn't go to any of the places the other students did, except for the library, but no one expected you to talk to them there, so it was safe. When I lied to myself, I said I didn't go to places like Kathryn's because I was too busy. I had two jobs and school. I had the soup kitchen, my regulars that I visited at St. Vincent's, and the old ladies at St. Paul's. And then there was Angel's office, where I still helped out when I could, though more often I just sat in the outside office and studied.

When I was being honest, I knew it was because I was scared to interact with the other students—even off campus.

I found it very different, being in Sophie's company. All the things that scared me seemed so inconsequential. She knew lots of the people at the café, and I fell into the easy cheerfulness I'd cultivated on the street. And you know what? It turned out that a smile and a kind word worked as well on college students as they did street people and the old folks at St. Vincent's. The students maybe didn't need it as much, but then who doesn't appreciate a bit of good spirits in their lives?

And as I let the conversations wash over me, I also found out that I wasn't the only student at Butler U. with problems. Theirs weren't the same as mine, but everybody had things they had to deal with, ranging from being on their own for the first time, to their course load, or the way some jerky guy had dumped them—that was the girls—or some skanky girl had led them on and then blown them off—and that was the boys.

But mostly the conversations centered around what we were studying. Art and poetry and literature. Movies and music. Pop culture and politics.

I didn't understand a lot of what I heard, but I liked to listen to it all, and kept rearranging the mental list in my head of what book I should read when I got a rare bit of spare time. What band I should go see. What gallery to visit.

The café itself lent itself to the easy camaraderie of the students. There were the tables and chairs one would expect—with Old World checkered tablecloths and candles stuck in empty Mateuse wine bottles—but there were also sofas and fat easy chairs, and even a pile of embroidered cushions in one corner. In another corner was a small stage where Sophie told me they had both music and poetry readings, mostly on the weekends. The walls carried an art show by a third year student—brilliantly overstated oils, full of way too much garish colour, that still totally worked. Apparently, there was a new show every month.

The bar was a long length of polished wood, and the wall behind it held matching shelves with a vast array of liquor bottles and glasses. On the lower counter there were coffee urns, others with hot water for tea, and even an espresso machine. Music played on the sound system—a mixtape of jazz, Latin rhythms, singer-songwriters and rock.

It was so different from the diner where I worked that it might as well have been another world. It *was* another world and at one point I leaned over to Sophie to tell her how happy I was that she'd brought me here. My guilt at cutting class had been reduced to just a niggle in the back of my mind. I didn't obsess over it because I knew I wasn't going to make a habit of it.

I'd noticed a help wanted sign on the way in and before I finally left to go to the Post Office for my evening shift, I got up my nerve to find the owner and apply. It turned out there really was a Kathryn—a big, cheerful woman in a loose cotton flowered hippie dress with hair down to her waist. She leaned her elbows on the counter and studied me for a long moment when I introduced my-self and asked for a job application form. After a moment, she turned her gaze to Sophie.

"Is this a friend of yours?"

Sophie nodded, then added to me, "Wendy works here part-time."

Kathryn laughed. "Everybody works here part-time except for Frank and me."

Frank was the cook, I found out later.

"Do you have any waiting experience?" she asked me.

I nodded, and told her about the diner.

"So when can you start?"

I blinked in surprise. Just like that?

"I…in a week or so," I said. "I have to give my notice at the diner." Then I added apologetically, "I don't want to leave them in the lurch. They were really good about hiring me without my having much experience."

Not to mention they knew I was a recovering junkie, but they still took a chance on me. That had been Angel's doing, putting in a good word for me.

"I like this girl," Kathryn told Sophie. "She has a sense of respon-sibility." Then she turned to me. "Come see me when you're done at the diner and we'll work up a schedule. You're at the university, I take it?"

I nodded. "First year fine arts."

"Of course you are. We don't exactly get many of the engineers in here."

She smiled and patted my hand, then went down the bar to take someone's order.

"This is so cool," Sophie said. "Maybe you can share some shifts with Wendy—you'll really like her."

And that was how I got over whatever it was that had been giving me the panic attacks whenever I came onto campus. It was so weird. It was as though I'd simply turned a page in a book and started a new story.

I didn't lie to any of these new friends of mine. That's what the junkie I'd been would have done. She'd have said or done anything to ingratiate herself with people, because she might be able to score a fix. Or steal something to sell for a fix. Whenever talk of my past came up, I'd just say I'd had an unhappy childhood and would just as soon not talk about it.

I said that a lot. And surprisingly, most people just let it go.

It took a long time for me to be able to trust civilians with the true sordid details—people like Sophie and Wendy.

Civilians. That's how street people thought of those who weren't like us. They were civilians in the war for survival. Citizens, while so many of us were barely scraping by. We were the hopeless and the lost, trapped by our addictions and inability to function in the world that they all just took for granted. We could see them from our alleys and gutters and squats, but we knew we could never be part of that world.

But now I was.

I really was.

It was a liberating and exhilarating feeling.

-7-

But that was then and this is now. Yes, Henry and I both reinvented ourselves, and we're both artists—or at least he is, and
I'm working on it—but those two similarities aren't enough for me to
open up to him about the sorry mess I once made of my life. Not
now. Maybe never. I don't know. It's too early to tell.

And then there's the big difference where he's dead and I'm not.

But he's waiting for me to reply to his comment about how I've
been there, all messed up, just like him.

So all I say is, "I guess we've got a lot in common—except for
the dying part."

He gets a strange look on his face.

"What?" I ask.

He shakes his head. "Nothing. Want me to show you around?"
he adds. "I can introduce you to some of the other artists and you
can pick out your studio space."

"Sounds great," I say. "Thanks."

It's late before I finally leave the warehouse. I have the streets to
myself as I make my way back to my apartment and fall asleep as soon
as my hits the pillow.

I start out the next morning for the bank, to get rent money for
the studio space and some art supplies, but just like last night, I find
myself back at the basketball court instead, where I first met Cholo

and his friends. The whole gang isn't there, but I spy Cholo sitting on a bench by the children's playground area, so I cross the asphalt and join him on the bench. He smiles hello, then turns back to look at the kids.

"I'm babysitting my niece Adriana," he explains, "and all she needs is three seconds of being unsupervised to get into trouble."

"That's nice of you."

He shrugs. "I like kids—*alto*, Adriana," he adds to his niece. "We don't kick other people."

Adriana is in the sandbox—a small version of Cholo with jet black hair, dark skin and those same mischievous eyes he has. She's stopped at the sound of his voice, her leg still in the air, then grins, does a pirouette and loses her balance. I wait for the tears when she falls into the sand, but she just brushes herself off and goes running off to the swings."

"*Perdón*," Cholo says to the woman Adriana had been about to kick.

"*Es nada*," she tells him and smiles.

Cholo looks at me for a moment. "There's something different about you today," he says before he turns to keep an eye on Adriana again.

"I washed my hair and my clothes are clean."

He grins, without turning. "That, too. No, it's something else. Like you're more *here* than you were the other night."

I thought he was going to say something about me having some kind of light—the way that Sophie always does. I don't believe there's any light—or rather, I don't believe it's in me. I think Sophie only sees a reflection of her own magical shine.

"I guess I'm fitting in," I say.

"I guess you are."

"So, should I call you Cholo or Gilbert?" I ask him.

"You can call me whatever you want."

"Yeah, but if 'cholo's' some kind of an insult…"

"Except it's not if you take it on yourself, you know what I mean? Then it becomes—what's the word? Empowering."

I'm not sure that's entirely true. When I was selling my body, I doubt calling myself a hooker would have empowered me. But I let it slide.

"You were telling me about some old men the other night," I say. "The ones that can go on for hours about what this place is."

"Yeah, they hang out at the park down the street. What do you want to ask them?"

"I don't know. How this all works, I guess. *Why* it all does."

"What does it matter? 'Scool, right? You were supposed to be dead, but you're not. Instead, you get a whole other life—a *better* life."

"Except I'm not dead."

He looks back from where his niece is swinging to study me for a moment.

"That's what's different," he says as he turns away again. "I could really tell the other night. Today?" He shrugs. "Not so much."

This doesn't strike me as such a good thing.

"Can you explain that a little more clearly?" I ask.

He shrugs again. "What's to explain? It's just something you see or you don't. Maybe it's easier to see in the dark, like it was the other night."

"So, these old guys," I say. "Anyone I should look for in particular?"

"Nah, they all love to talk. Especially to a pretty *muchacha*. The trick'll be getting them to shut up."

His gaze returns to me when I stand up.

"You're going already?" he asks.

I nod.

"So what about us, you know…hanging sometime when I'm not babysitting and you're not in a hurry?"

I smile. "That could happen."

"Ah, you're a tough one, are you?"

"No. I'm just not finished hurrying yet."

"Well, you know where to find me."

"Is she supposed to be doing that?" I ask

I point to where Adriana is standing on the seat of the swing and trying to climb up one of the support ropes.

"*Ay, mira!*" he cries and runs over to his niece before she can take a tumble.

"I'll see you later," I call over when he's got her safely in his arms.

He sets Adriana down onto the sand and waves to me. I wave back, then set off down the street to where he told me I'd find the park.

The park would be a beautiful little oasis of green in the middle of all the concrete if it weren't for the fact that the street is lined with trees—tall, old elms, untouched by disease like all the ones we lost back home. There's a big fountain in the middle, the water spewing from an urn that some cherubic looking fellow is holding, and there's almost a couple of dozen old men, scattered on the various benches.

It's funny, I got the impression from Cholo that they'd all be Hispanic, and there are a few, but there are also blacks, East Europeans, Lebanese, Italians—all sorts. There are so many that I don't know where to start. But since most of them are sitting in groups of two or three, I pick an old fellow who's on a nearby bench by himself.

He sits with a stoop in his shoulders, elbows on the knees of his worn dress trousers as he stares off into the distance. He has a full head of long grey hair, combed back from his brow, and one of those noses that are hooked like a hawk's beak, but give the features a noble cast—or at least it would if this fellow had bothered to shave in the past few days. Still, who am I to talk about scruffy?

I approach his bench and see that he's looking inward, rather than at anything I or anybody else could see. I clear my throat, but get no response.

"Hello?" I try.

He doesn't look up for so long that I'm sure he didn't hear me. But just when I'm about to repeat myself, he lifts his face and his gaze meets mine.

"Piss off," he says.

Then he spits a stream of tobacco juice on the pavement near my feet.

I have to laugh.

"What's so funny?"

"Nothing, really. It's just that you're the first person I've met here who hasn't been all…oh, I don't know. In a good mood at least."

"Yeah, well welcome to hell."

"Hell? That's the last word I'd use to describe this place."

"What would you call it?"

"It seems pretty much perfect, don't you think? I mean, everything just seems to fall in your lap. You need a place to stay, and there's an apartment for you. You need money, well, you don't have to work, because here's this fat bank account. At least that's the way it's working out for me so far."

Now it was the old man's turn to laugh. "Thank god I was never that naïve."

I sit down on the bench beside him.

"So tell me about it," I say.

"No. Now piss off."

"But I want to hear your story."

"I don't have a story," he tells me.

"Then tell me the story of this city. Tell me why my impression of it is so naïve."

"You know you're dead, right?" he says.

"Well, I'm not, but I get that most people here are."

He shakes his head. It's obvious that he's about to say one thing, but I can see him change his mind.

"This guy I met when I got here," he says. "He told me this is the city of the unfulfilled dead. I don't mean that's what it's called. That's just what it *is*. It's the place people come when they've died unexpectedly, before their time. When they believe they haven't had the chance to leave their mark on the world, and make something of their life. So they're not ready to move on."

"Move on to where?"

"We don't know that here anymore than we did before we died."

"But don't most people die before they're ready? I mean, I know there are people who are sick and everything, but I'd think that everybody still feels they have something to contribute and aren't ready to die."

"I suppose. I don't how it works. There are a lot of theories. Some believe that there are all kinds of different worlds in the afterlife— places for innocents, places for suicides, others for people who die in accidents. Some are closer to the world of the living than others, some are all the way on the other side of whatever. The going theory about this place we're in is that if you wasted your life, or meant to do this special thing with it, but never got around to it, here's the place you get a second chance. You talk to anybody here and they fit the criteria."

I nod, thinking of people I've met so far. Donna, Cholo, Henry.

"But there's a big flat flaw to that theory," the old man goes on. "Either that, or whatever runs this place isn't as astute as you'd want, or expect, something in its position to be."

He pauses long enough that I realize he's expecting something from me.

"Why's that?" I ask.

"I was done with life before I died and I'm sure as hell done with it again in this damn place. Yeah, anything you want's here for the taking. But leaving isn't. Or at least I haven't figured how to get out."

"But why would you want to leave?"

"Call me stubborn, but I don't like anybody—or any*thing*—deciding what I'm going to do with my life. Or rather, my death."

"And you've tried?"

He nods. "A couple of years ago, I just started walking down Princess Boulevard there." He points to the street I took to get here from where I left Cholo with his niece. "It took me six months, but you know where I ended up?"

I shake my head.

"Right back here."

"You're saying this whole world is one big city?"

He shrugs. "Maybe I got turned around. I was on Princess the whole time, and it sure seemed to go straight, but who knows? I could have been walking in circles, except the sun kept rising straight in front of me, so I know I was walking east the whole time. Unless this place has different rules about the compass directions. But the point is, this city is big."

If what he's saying is true, it's enormous.

"I'll say," I tell him.

"And there's no way out."

He spits some more tobacco juice, but this time it's in the opposite direction from where I'm sitting.

"Out," I say. "You mean back?"

"Back or on to whatever's next—it doesn't matter to me. I just don't want to be *here*."

"I came here through the door of a club," I tell him.

"You died in a club?"

"No. I was supposed to meet a friend at this club in Newford—that's the city where I live."

"I know where Newford is, kid."

"Right. Anyway, it was this club on Lee Street that no one I know had ever heard of before, but there it was all the same, so I went in. And you know, it seemed pretty normal—just a bar with good music. But when the show was over and we stepped outside, we were here instead."

He cocks his head, gaze still skeptical, but considering now.

"So you're really alive?" he says.

I nod.

"Funny. You've got a really settled-in look about you."

"I've only been here a couple of days."

"Okay," he says, "so maybe I buy that. But what the hell are you still doing here? Wake up, or do whatever it takes to get out this place. What's the matter with you?"

"Well, my friend Donna—it was her band I went to see. She thinks I should stay."

He shakes his head. "No, the way it really works is, she *has* to stay, so she wants you to as well."

"That's not true. Why would you say that?"

"Because it's what the dead do. We want to surround ourselves with pieces of our past. It makes us feel more alive. It makes it easier to believe that this place isn't a lie."

I remember how that came up when I was talking to Donna's brother, this idea that everything we could see around us was just a façade.

"So where are we really?" I ask. "If this isn't real, then what is it?"

"I didn't say it wasn't real," he tells me. "I'm saying it's only real if you want it to be. Or need it to be. Which is great, I suppose, unless you're somebody like me who doesn't want or need it."

I shake my head. "Something's real or it's not. It can't be both."

"And that's why you're naïve," he says. "Let me put it another way," he adds at my frown. "Everything is made of layers—like an onion—and you have to keep peeling back the layers to get to the truth—not just the paper skin on the outside, but all of them. But here's the funny thing. What's true for you might not be true for me."

"That doesn't make sense," I say.

"Maybe, maybe not. But it's the way of the world, kid. Everything's just like you see it—simple and direct with no bullshit. But if you think about it too much, and you get a bunch of people talking about it, then it all gets so complicated that nothing can make sense. It's all in how you look at it. It's all in how we all agree it is."

"This is such bullshit."

"You want to hear some real truths? Go to the canal tonight and listen to the whispers."

"I was warned not to do that."

He nods. "Yeah, there'll always be people who try to keep you from what you need to know."

"Like you?"

He spits another stream of tobacco juice onto the pavement and smiles when I pull a face.

"Now I'm done talking," he says, "so get out of here."

I nod and stand up. I'm done, too. He's been so depressing I want to go have a drink. Not a social drink—say, a beer, like I had with Donna and her friends the other night. But a real drink. Whiskey or tequila. Something to change the way I'm feeling. But I know where that'll take me and I'm not going there anymore.

I look around the park. I have no energy to try to talk to any of the other old men. But I need to get away from this depressing old man. Whatever amusement I got over his crankiness in this city of cheerful—if early-to-bed—people has long since worn off.

I have no intention of going to the canal, either, but you know how it is. We let the good things slide right out of our minds, but a depressing thought or an anxiety—*that* we hang onto and worry at for so long that we can't ever let it go.

I know the old man's full of crap, but I keep thinking back to when I was in Donna and Tommy's apartment the other night, when Tommy and I were wondering if all of this—this city and everything in it—was just a façade, and if it was, what was behind it.

I know that Donna would never do anything to hurt me, but the Donna I knew wasn't covered with tattoos. She didn't play bass in a rockabilly band or ride a motorcycle. More to the point, she'd been *alive*. So who was to say something else might not have changed?

I know that whatever's going on at the canal is something I should avoid. I saw what it did to Cholo's friend Petey. Whatever he'd heard or seen that night had been eating him up.

I hate this. I can feel the old familiar depression taking hold of me again and even though this place and the possibility of my life here seems perfect, I start to obsess on all the ways things could go wrong. I'm so caught up in this stupid tangle of thoughts that I don't realize I'm in the middle of a crowd until someone says:

"Why so glum, chum?"

I snap back to my surroundings the way you pop out of a really intense dream, disoriented and blinking, pulse quick—

And feel like I've woken up in the middle of a carnival.

I'm surrounded by people in colourful costumes—I think there's about a dozen of them, but it's hard to tell because of how they keep moving around. There are ribbons fluttering everywhere, tasseled hats, hair as wild as my own, oversized shirts over dancers' tights, flapping clown pants below skin-tight, tie-dyed T-shirts. It's a riot of colour and movement, because not one of them is standing still. Some are dancing, keeping time with their jangling tambourines and the anklets of bells that many of them are wearing. Others are doing acrobatics. Two of them are on short stilts, but are still able to do a kind of tap-dance on the pavement.

And then there are the dogs. I spy almost as many of them as there are people, mutts mostly, of every size and description. They, too, are festooned with ribbons and bows, and run in among the people, barking and yipping and adding to the general hubbub.

I focus on the woman directly in front of me, the one who spoke. She has long blonde hair festooned with coloured ribbons and beads, and her eyes are so blue it's like staring into the sky when you meet her gaze. Her jacket appears to be made entirely of fluttering strips of cloth, each with a bell on the end, so that she jingles with every move she makes. And like the others, she's constantly moving, jigging in place and grinning at me.

"Who are you people?" I say.

"Such a question!" she says. "We're improvateers—what else could we be?"

"Yes, but—"

She holds up a hand. "We need two words from you, but those won't do. Preferably a pair of nouns, but a verb will do in a pinch."

"I don't understand."

She shakes her head. "That's three words, and they're much too vague. Try again."

Her companions take up her last words and turn them into a swirling madrigal that swoops and rises in perfect harmonies.

"Try again, try again, try again…"

"Give us two words," the blonde woman tells me, "and in return, we'll give you a story. A song. A dance. A play. We'll fill the park with drama and joy, because that's what we do."

"Because we're improvateers," her chorus cries and then they begin to sing again: "Improvateers, improvateers, like buccaneers, though not so feared."

One short fellow starts doing cartwheels. The woman and man on stilts are doing a rather graceful cancan dance in time to the song. The rest gather into a group, clasp hands against their breasts, and sing with earnest fervor, while the dogs race around and around them.

I can't help but laugh. Their general mayhem is putting everything out of my mind: the canal, the old man, going to the bank, getting art supplies, the studio space, *everything*. I still don't know what this world is, or what my place in it will be, but at this moment, I don't care.

"Milady?" the blonde asks, her eyebrows rising to add emphasis.

I've taken to thinking of her as Jingles because she has more bells than any of them and their sound accentuates her every motion.

I say the first words that pop into my head. "Um…hedgehogs and cheese?"

Jingles grins and gives me an elaborate bow.

"Excellent choice," she says. Then she turns to her companions. "Milady has chosen the story of the Hedgehog Who Kept the Deed to Her Burrow in a Wedge of Cheese. Shall we begin?"

I'm not sure what the ensuing madness has to do with hedgehogs or cheese, but the two words come up time and time again and the whole thing is vastly entertaining. There are dances and dramatic scenes, songs and heartfelt soliloquies, and for a grand finale, the whole troupe forms a pyramid with the pair on stilts bookending them on either side.

Quite a crowd has gathered by the end of finale and the members of the troupe go among them with hats in hand, collecting donations. Even a few of the dogs are carrying hats in their mouths, weaving in and around the crowd. I reach into my pocket, but then remember I haven't been to the bank yet.

"I'm sorry," I tell Jingles who's come back to stand near me. "I don't have any money on me. But that was fantastic."

"Pish posh," she says. "You were our muse, our inspiration, our very reason for gathering such a potent and wondrous performance from the dribbles and drabbles of our own weak imaginations."

I smile. "I only gave you two words."

"But such compelling and intoxicating words they were. They held in them all the resonance and drama of a tale that could only take on mythic proportions, given its inspired origin. Don't deny it—you saw the wonder unfold with your very own eyes."

"I saw something wonderful, all right, but I still don't think I had much to do with it."

"Milady, you wound me with your humility. You had everything to do with it. In fact, we improvateers are so indebted to you that I insist you join us for refreshment now that our day's performance is done."

"My name's Jilly," I tell her.

She reaches out a hand. "Rebecca Rebecca, at your service."

I smile as I shake. "Rebecca Rebecca?"

"My parents liked the name so much that they used it twice."

"And do you ever turn it off?" I ask.

"Not really," she says and winks. "And certainly not in public."

She turns to the rest of the troupe who are consolidating their earnings from many hats into one large handbag in the shape of an alligator. It looks like it's made of fabric maché and has the words "I am not a handbag" inscribed on either side.

"Come, come," Rebecca Rebecca tells them. "We have a guest for our evening repast, so homeward all. The dillys that dally shall have to sleep in an alley."

Then she hooks her arm in mine and off we go, deeper into the park, the troupe falling in with us, some lagging behind, others ranging ahead with the dogs, all of them taking turns singing the verses of some ridiculous song continuing the adventures of a hedgehog who stores her valuables in a safe made of cheese.

It turns out that the part of the park where I first came in, with the cherub fountain and old men, is only the very tip of a green space that takes up almost forty acres. There are forests and meadows, Rebecca Rebecca tells me, a small lake, hills, two streams, all of it interlaced with a spider's web of pedestrian and bike paths. The improvateers have a camp on the western edge of the park where it backs onto a military base that's no longer in service.

Like the improvateers themselves, the camp is a hodgepodge of carnival tents and teepees, all bright primary colours with flags and pennants rising high above the canvas. It's a cheerful, joyous place—much like its inhabitants—and I find myself remembering Donna talking about Utopias where everyone pitches in, where it's the headspace of the people that makes the difference, so that rules aren't necessary. Here, it actually seems to be working, because as soon as they arrive, everybody peels off their gaudy clothes and pitches in to make dinner.

"So, Rebecca Rebecca," I begin

"Just one Rebecca's fine—think of it as a nickname."

I smile and go on. "So, Rebecca, then. How can I help?"

"Pish, posh. You're our guest. What kind of hosts would we be if we made our guests work for their supper?"

"The kind that lets guests pitch in?"

"Well, if you put it like that…"

The meal tonight is a big spread of brown rice and various vegetables and breads that were acquired from the back of groceries and restaurants that would have otherwise been thrown out. The first thing that goes on the fire is a big pot to boil water and soon the scent of some heavenly aromatic tea comes drifting over to where we're all cutting vegetables for the stew and salads.

I've been introduced to everybody, but it's such a blur of names that I don't have a hope of remembering them all. There's whistling and humming, a few songs. The dogs play some mad game of chase, around and around our feet, hoping for scraps.

"There's something about you…" Rebecca says, cutting celery beside me.

"Yes, I know. I'm this terrifically inspiring muse."

Rebecca grins. "That, too. No, you've got a glow about you. I was never one for the whole aura business—but then," she adds, "I wasn't one to believe in life after death, either. Until I ended up here. Big wake-up call."

I hadn't told her yet.

"I'm not dead," I say and go on to describe how I got here.

"I guess that explains the way it's like your aura's pushing out of your skin the way it does."

I think of Sophie and feel the twinge of homesickness I get whenever I think of any of my friends.

"And I guess it also explains," Rebecca goes on, "why you seem to have this light about you. I got the same thing when I first arrived here."

I give her a surprised look. "You didn't die, either?"

"Nope. I got an invitation from a friend—Benny there." She points to a reed-thin man with brown curls as long and wild as my own, except his are tamed back into the semblance of a ponytail. He's on the rice-making detail. "And he didn't so much as invite me here as to the opening of a play. I met him in the foyer of a theatre I'd never heard of before, saw this amazing performance piece, and when we exited out one of the stage doors, here we were."

"That's like what happened to me."

She nods. "I think it's kind of required for those of us who didn't actually die. We get an invitation, but we make the decision as to whether or not we'll take it up. And then, of course, we decide again whether or not we'll stay."

"Have you been here a long time?"

"A couple of years. I was so heartbroken when Benny died. We weren't lovers, but we were the best of friends. Inseparable, until he was diagnosed with bone cancer. Wait," she adds. "That came out wrong. I mean, we were inseparable until he died. I was with him right through all the treatments."

"That must have been so horrible."

"It was. And then...well, it was even worse when he died. I thought I'd be a little better, not having to see him going through all he did and being in such pain. You know, for his sake?"

I nod.

"But instead this big hole opened up inside me and I just couldn't pull myself out again. Until I got here."

"So I don't have to ask if you're happy."

"It's not a matter of being happy or not," she says. "It's a matter of being fulfilled. Back home—on the other side." She laughs. "I still don't know what to call it. I don't want to say something like the land of the living because everybody here seems way more alive than they did back there. Anyway, I was just working in an office, always dreaming of being able to do something like this."

She makes a grand gesture with her whole arm to take in all of the camp.

"And here I can," she finishes.

"Did you know everybody else before?" I ask.

She shakes her head. "Cindy, Theodore." She points them out as she names them. "And of course Benny. The rest are just new friends of like mind."

"And do you do your improv in the park every day?"

"Oh no. That would be so boring. We go everywhere and anywhere. We've been at this camp for a few months now. One day we'll just pack everything up again and go to another part of the city."

"Does it have an end?" I ask. "The city, I mean. I was talking to an old guy who said he walked for a few months, always keeping the sun rising in front of him, but he still ended up back at the same place. It was like the city took up the whole surface of the planet."

"Unless the physics are different here. There's so much else that's different."

"That's true."

"So this guy you were talking to," she says. "Was he really cranky? Did he have a real hawk's nose? Sat by himself, dressed in a suit and could use a shave?"

I nod.

"That's Gus. I've tried talking to him a few times, but he just brings me down."

"He's not the most cheerful sort," I agree.

"Exactly. But meeting him did make me feel that all of this is really real. That I didn't, you know, have an episode or something and was simply dreaming all of this from a padded cell back home." She gives me a crooked smile. "My depression got really bad."

"It's weird how it just feeds on itself, isn't it?"

"So you've been there."

I nod. "Except I used drugs to make it…not so much better. More like bearable"

"I hear you. So you must have been as happy to find yourself here as I was."

"I like it here," I tell her, "but I'd been pretty much done with all the crap in my life before I ran into my friend Donna again."

"Good for you."

"But getting back to Gus," I say. "How did meeting him make this more real for you?"

She nods. "Because he's always so grumpy—and he's not the only one. I've met a few others like him."

"I don't get it."

"If it was all just sunshine and light, all the people, all the time, well, that would make it too much like some happy dream that I was only escaping into."

"Of course."

I'm about to ask her if she's ever been to the canal, but then supper's ready and between the wonderful food and drink, the conversations and tomfoolery going on all around me, I never get back to it.

It's late in the evening when the meal's done and everything's been cleaned up and put away. The improvateers are very conscientious about not leaving their garbage around. The dogs are already all asleep. By ones and twos, the people go to their tents until finally I'm sitting by the fire with only Rebecca and this delightful black man named Tripper—"I used to do a lot of drugs," he told me when we were introduced for the second time and I actually remembered his name enough to ask him about it. He's got an infectious laugh and his teeth are so white that they do a Cheshire Cat thing whenever he grins. Which is often.

"You can bunk with Benny and me," Rebecca says when Tripper finally says goodnight and heads off to his own bed.

"No, that's okay," I tell her. "I'll go back to my apartment. I really need to make a fresh start in the morning and get some things done."

"You can find your way?"

I nod. "And it's not like it's dangerous. Why does everyone go to bed so early? It seems so weird for a city this size."

"I don't know. Maybe it's like a Disneyland thing—or any carnival or circus."

"What do you mean?"

"It's chaos at the end of the show, but come morning, everything's sparkly and clean again. I figure there are little gnomes or something running around at night, putting everything in order again for the next day."

"Really?"

Because I'm getting ready to believe anything these days.

She laughs. "Maybe. Who knows? I'm never up long enough to find out. Maybe you'll see them on the way home and you can come back and tell me."

"It's a deal," I say.

I've been doing little sketches all evening. Now I put my sketchbook away and stand up.

"If I see any gnomes," I add, "you'll be the first person I'll tell."

She stands up with me.

"You're sure you don't want to stay over?"

"No, I'll be fine. I've got a good sense of direction, and there's nothing scary, right?"

"No. There's just…"

"Just what?" I ask when she doesn't pick up from where her voice trailed off.

"Nothing, really. It's just better to avoid large bodies of water at night."

"Like the canal."

She nods. "Good. You've already been warned. Apparently, man-made waterways are the more powerful conduits."

"Have you heard the whispers?" I ask.

She nods again, but doesn't elaborate.

"Was it really horrible?"

"Pretty much. It makes you question everything you did with your life, and what you're doing with what you have now."

"What if you're already doing that?" I ask.

"Then I guess it'll just be that much more intense—and harder to bear. If you stay too long—and it's so very difficult to break away, once you start listening—everything begins to seem horrible and pointless. All you want to do is…"

She suddenly shakes her head, then grins at me and the woman I'd first met in the park is in her place.

"Pish, posh," she says. "Why are we being all doom and gloomy? You're the happy artist-in-waiting and I'm an improvateer! Not for us the wormy words of the wily water. I've no intention of going back, and you've no intention of going in the first place, wiser woman you, so what care we?"

I want to press her, but even with only the firelight to see by, I can tell that her smile is too bright, her sudden high spirits forced. She's scared, I realize. Scared of what she remembers. Knowing that, how can I try to make her keep talking?

"That's me," I say. "Wise woman and muse. My rates are cheap."

She lays a hand on my arm. "You'll be sure to take care."

"My dear," I tell her. "Care is, in fact, my middle name."

I don't add that, need be, I can be as falsely jolly as the best improvateer.

"Thanks for everything," I add. "I'll be back—unless you've plans to move on soon?"

"No. We'll be here for a week or two."

She gives me a hug and I concentrate on not being stiff. I even manage to hug her back and swear to myself that no matter what else I get up to in this new life of mine, I'm going to teach myself to be a little less uptight about my personal space. People like Rebecca aren't my brother or any of the other freaks who hurt me. They don't deserve to be treated with wariness.

We hug a last time, then I set off on the path that will take me back to Princess Boulevard. I look back once, just before the camp is lost from view, and I see her still standing there in the firelight, watching me, though I doubt she can see me anymore. The night's dark here, out of the camp, the path is unlit, and my shape would be lost against the darker bulk of the forest.

There's enough starlight for me to differentiate the path from the lawn, but I lose that, too, once I'm walking under the trees. I have to slow down and walk with one foot on the asphalt, the other on the grass, just to make sure I keep on the path.

I go through another field, another wood. The way seemed much shorter with a gaggle of improvateers and dogs. But then when I come out of a third wood, shuffling along on the edge of the path, I see lamps ahead of me. A few minutes later and I'm back in the area where I first met Rebecca and her friends. It takes me a moment to orient myself—I got here from where I'd been talking with Gus in a kind of a daze, not really noticing where I was going—but then I get my bearings and head off, back toward my apartment.

The streets are deserted, of course. I find myself looking for goblins or whatever it is that looks after things in the city at night, but there's only me, my shoes scuffing on the pavement. I smile at my foolishness, but then I hear a sound I can't place.

I stop to listen. It's not the thump of a basketball, and I'm not near the basketball court anyway. This is different. Subtler. It's more like a rustle or a murmur. Secretive, but seductive, too.

A picture pops into my head of little goblins and fairy men, a foot high or smaller, pushing tiny twig brooms, putting trash into moleskin sacks, and though I know it's just more foolishness— too much time spent in the company of improvateers mixed with my own overactive imagination—I turn off Princess Boulevard to follow the sound.

I walk as quietly as I can so as not to give myself away, but I shouldn't have bothered. A few blocks and a couple of turns later I stop dead in my tracks and stare at what lies before me.

It's a bridge.

Old stonework, a gentle slope going up before it descends on the other end with a fat balustrade on either side. The lamps on the cast iron posts are electric, but they mimic old gas lamps like I've seen in pictures of Newford back in the early 1900s.

But it's not the bridge that stops me and makes my pulse go into quicktime.

It's what the bridge goes over:

The canal. The dark water that runs under the old stonework. Dark water filled with insistent whispers that I can almost, but not quiet make out. Except for one word.

My name.

Jilly.

Jilly.

I don't want to go any closer and hear what the whispers are saying.

But I can't *not* go either.

I've always had too much cat in me. I always need to find out the real story. See things for myself.

I need to *know*.

Even now. Even when I've been told, over and over again, how horrible it will be.

I still need to know.

I start to approach before I'm completely aware of doing it. I walk up to the end of the bridge, then turn down the side and follow a steep grassed slope to the edge of the canal. The water is high, no more than a foot below the stone wall that drops into its dark depths and holds the canal to its shape. There's a fence made up of a single railing to keep people from falling in.

I kneel on the stone. I could easily reach in and touch the water, but I don't. I lean against the metal rail and look down. There should be reflections on the surface—the bright lamps up on the bridge, if nothing else—but it's all dark.

And now I can start to make out what the whispers are saying, and I understand how their words can be both horrible and tell the truth. Because I'm hearing my friends, the ones I left behind. They must be all together somewhere.

They…

"…believe she did this," Sophie is saying. *"She told me how hard she'd worked to get clean. She was so happy—didn't you think she was happy?"*

"A lot happier than when I first met her," Geordie says. *"I watched her blossom from this scared kid to the cheerful woman we've all come to know and love."*

"You'd think she would have talked to one of us," Wendy says. *"We could have helped her."*

"Maybe she didn't trust us," Sophie says.

"More likely she's too ashamed."

That was Angel.

"But we'd stick by her," Sophie says.

"And we wouldn't judge her," Wendy adds.

"We need to find her," Sophie says. *"Where do you think she'd go?"*

"She used to live in these squats in the Tombs," Geordie says.

"So we'll go find her," Wendy says.

"We can't bring her back," Angel says.

"Are you crazy?" Sophie says. *"We have to. We can't just leave her out there on her own."*

But, *"Why not?"* Wendy asks, talking to Angel.

"Because it doesn't work that way," Angel says. *"You can't make somebody go clean, or stay clean. They have to want to. We can be there to support her, but she has to decide she's ready to come back."*

"I hate this," Sophie says. *" I can't stand the idea of her lying in an alley somewhere, all strung out on dope with no one to help her".*

"I hate it, too," Angel says. *" I never thought Jilly would disappoint me like this. But it's not even me so much. I can't believe she'd let herself down this badly. It's funny. In the back of your mind, you always half-expect this kind of thing, but I never did with Jilly. She seemed so determined to change things around for herself. And she had so much to give."*

"She promised me," Sophie says. "She promised she'd never desert me the way my mother did. Why did I believe her?"

This is worse than I could ever have imagined. And those voices aren't alone. I hear Kathryn at the café, wondering why I've missed so many shifts. I hear the ladies at the church, my co-workers at the soup kitchen, the old ladies and old men at St. Vincent's, where the care-workers try to explain my absence. I hear Angel and Lou having a different conversation from the one Angel was having with Sophie, Wendy and Geordie. I hear them all talking, together, in pairs, in threes.

Talking and talking and talking.

They all know I've just blown them off. That I won't be coming back.

They think I've gone back to my old life. That I'm tattooing track marks on my arms again as I sink back into oblivion.

But the truth is almost worse. The truth is I've tossed them aside to make this pretty little perfect life for myself here. Here, where you don't have to work at anything. It's just given to you.

And Sophie. Sophie.

I *did* promise her.

My heart breaks and I'm so ashamed.

I hang on the railing, my tears spilling into the water. I can't bear this. I need to get away, but I can't move.

All I can do is listen.

-8-

The first time I met Wendy was outside of Kathryn's Café, just before my first shift. She was on her break, and though there was a brisk nip in the autumn air, she was sitting at one of the patio tables, scribbling in the journal she carried everywhere, just like I did my sketchbook. She was hunched over the pages, her curly blonde hair falling in a torrent to either side of her face.

I didn't know her then, or even that she was writing. I thought she was sketching, and since I still had a few minutes before my shift started, I walked over to her table to see what had captured her interest so much that she was sitting out here in the chill to get it down on paper.

See what I mean? I was off-campus, so whatever anxiety it was that clamped around my chest and made it hard for me to even look someone in the face, wasn't present. I could be like I was in Angel's neighbourhood. Cheerful and happy to talk to anyone.

Sophie, in the few days that I'd known her, had been helping me integrate these two warring sides of my personality, but I could still get tight inside, and go all quiet, when we stepped off West Stanton Street and onto the quad.

"What are you drawing…?" I started to say, then broke off because I was close enough to see that those were words she was putting down on paper, not lines to capture shape and light. "Oh, I'm sorry," I quickly added. "I didn't realize you were writing."

She lifted her head and brushed a tangle of blonde curls from out of her face.

"That's okay," she said. "Just let me finish this line."

She wrote a few more words, then closed the book and laid her pen down on top of it.

"I should just go," I said. "I really didn't want to interrupt you."

"And you really aren't. All I had was four lines that I kept repeating to myself until it was time for my break when I could write them down. And I did. But now?" She held her palms open between us. "Now I've got nothing."

"You work here at Kathryn's?"

She nodded. "And it's been really busy. Lisa—the other waitress who was supposed to take this evening shift called in with a migraine, so I'm stuck working two back-to-back. Just me and a new girl who starts tonight. God, I hope she has some experience."

"That would be me," I tell her.

"You're Jilly?"

I nod. "And I do have experience—but in a diner, not a café. I've never used an espresso machine."

"Kathryn didn't show you around?"

"No, she just told me to come in for this shift."

Wendy shook her head. "She can be such a ditz."

I didn't want to start putting down the woman who'd given me the chance to get away from the grease and bright lights of the diner to work in a cool place like this.

"I like her," I said.

"Are you kidding?" Wendy said. "She's an absolute doll. But sometimes she's a little vague on the details, like telling you what you're supposed to do, or at least showing you how to run the espresso machine. Come on," she added, standing up. "Let me give you a quick crash course before Karen leaves. Once she's gone it'll just the two of us on the floor because Andy never comes out of the kitchen. I swear the guy is having a love affair with the fridge or something."

The next couple of hours were more hectic than the breakfast shift at the diner, but we got through it. I felt sorry for Wendy, though, because here she was, coming off the busy dinner shift and having to work twice as hard because I didn't have the hang of anything yet and the place was full of students, everybody wanting a drink of one sort or another.

I was okay with serving beer and wine, though it was weird having to ask to see I.D. all the time. At least nobody asked for a mixed drink. But I was a total klutz on the espresso machine. I never realized what a fine art it was to make the perfect cappuccino or café au lait.

It finally slowed down a little around ten—not because we didn't have customers. It was more that most of the students were like me, on a budget, and were nursing their drinks.

"So what do you think?" Wendy asked.

We were both leaning on the bar, looking out at the crowd as we appreciated the lull.

"About what?"

"Working here."

"Well, the tips aren't great," I said, "but I like it. The place has such a great atmosphere."

"I know. I hang out here half the time when I'm not working. Which—let me warn you in advance—can be slightly dangerous if Kathryn suddenly decides she needs another waitress on the floor and, oh how convenient, there you just happen to be."

"So she's a tough boss?"

Wendy shook her head. "No. Like I said, she's a doll. But she also knows she's running a business and isn't above taking advantage of our goodwill."

I went off to refill a girl's coffee.

"So what's your major?" Wendy asked when I returned.

"Fine art. What about you?"

"Journalism. My true love is poetry, but you can't exactly make a living at it. I thought my parents would die of shock when they saw I was doing something practical. But I figure I still get to take lots of English courses and I pretty much like any kind of writing anyway. I've always got words fluttering around in my head."

"Sounds like me and drawing, except while I can see how it should be, I can never quite get it to come out right once I start drawing or painting."

"That's what we're here to learn."

I nodded. "You sound like Sophie. She gave me the pep talk I needed a week or so ago."

"I know. She told me about meeting you. And then you got her to skip class. You have to tell me how you managed that. She'll never do it with me."

"I think she just felt sorry for me. I was feeling pretty down and just couldn't face going into class."

Wendy pretended to make a note of that, writing on the counter with an imaginary pencil.

"Got it," she said. "Look like you're feeling down. Make her feel sorry for you."

"It wasn't like that…"

"I'm *kidding*. So were you having boyfriend troubles?"

"I don't have a boyfriend. It was more like…it was an anxiety attack."

She put her hand on my arm. "Oh, I'm sorry. Now I feel like a bully. Just ignore me—I'm always running on at the mouth."

"No, it's okay. I didn't have the most orthodox upbringing so I'm still kind of learning my way around…"

Ordinary people, I want to say, but I just leave it hanging instead.

I could tell that Wendy wanted to ask about what I meant by an unorthodox upbringing, but she changed the subject instead.

"Do you have Professor Dapple?" she asked.

"For art history, and one of my life drawing classes, although he doesn't seem to actually draw, himself."

"I have him for art history, too, but not in the same course as you, obviously. Isn't he a doll?"

That was obviously one of her favourite words, but it fit the professor with his mad halo of white hair and small stature, always gesturing with a pipe in one hand while he pushed up his glasses with the other.

"Did you know that he lives in this huge mansion on Stanton Street?" she went on. "Not on the university side of the river, but on the east, where all the posh houses are."

I knew just the area she was talking about. I walked there sometimes, admiring the houses. Stanton Street was lined with giant oak trees which were often full of crows, but they made pretty much the only noise in the area. Even the traffic seemed hushed on Stanton.

"I guess his family had money," I said.

Because a professor's salary wouldn't pay for one of the houses there.

Wendy shook her head. "No, it's from his books. He's written gads of them."

"On art?"

"Some, sure. But mostly on folklore and fairy tales and the mythologies of the Kickaha Indians."

She went on to tell me about a couple that she'd read and we spent the rest of our shift looking after customers and talking about the mutual love it turned out we both had for fairy tales. She still had her copy of *The Wandering Wood* by Ellen Wentworth, which had been my best, and often only, friend while growing up.

We were still talking about it after we were closed and we busied ourselves getting the café ready for tomorrow morning.

The best thing about these new friends of mine was that they all got along famously with each other. Well, Sophie and Wendy were already friends, but they both adored Geordie—each of them taking me aside at one point or another insisting that he and I were perfect for other, but I didn't listen. Geordie and I knew that wasn't for us. Or at least I did. It wasn't something I ever discussed with him.

They all got along with Angel, too, and soon Sophie was helping me with the ladies at St. Paul's, while Wendy started volunteering at St. Vincent's Home for the Aged. And we all pitched in at the soup kitchen, though I was the only one to find the time a couple of times every week.

The only thing I found frustrating was that I didn't have a place to work on my art away from Butler U. I had things I wanted to try, but I still felt self-conscious attempting them in such public places as the studios at the university, and I couldn't really set up a big easel and start painting in my little bedroom in the rooming house. But I couldn't afford studio space either.

Sophie was in the same boat, as me, making ends meet with student loans and part-time work, which didn't allow for the luxury of a studio. But then a wonderful thing happened. We were talking about it with each other—as we often did—while cleaning up after one of our life drawing courses, when Professor Dapple came up to us.

"I couldn't help but overhear the two of you," he said, "and I think I might have a solution. That is, if you can put up with my very cantankerous housekeeper."

We both looked blank.

"I have an unused greenhouse in the back of my place," he explained. "It's heated and has running water, and the only thing we use it for is wintering geraniums. There'd be plenty of space to set up a couple of easels and if you make a mess, well, it would be easy to clean up. You can simply hose the floor down."

"Are you serious?" Sophie asked.

"Completely. I'm sure I even have a couple of old easels lying about. I'll have Goon—that's my housekeeper, Olaf Goonasekara, actually, but he insists on being called Goon, God knows why. I'll have him bring them up. You could start to set up your studio space tomorrow afternoon. Do know the address?"

We'd both been standing there with our mouths open. Sophie managed to shake her head.

"Here, let me find a card," he said.

He rummaged around in the pockets of his tweed jacket until he found one. He handed it to Sophie.

"It'll be your space," he said, "and you can do what you want in it, but I do recommend you keep it somewhat tidy or you'll certainly hear about it from Goon. He'll take it as a personal affront that any part of the house is untidy—Lord knows, I have enough trouble keeping him from reorganizing my library. Every time he does, it takes me weeks to be able to find anything again."

He looked from Sophie to me.

"You do want the space, don't you?" he asked.

"Oh, yes," I said quickly. I was still overcome with my surprise at his generosity, but not so much that I was going to let this opportunity slip by. "Thank you so much."

"Nonsense. You both have a great deal of talent and all the thanks I'll want is that you fulfill the potential I see in you."

He saw potential in us? I thought. Well, with Sophie, that was a given. But he saw it in me, too?

"We'll do our very best," I told him. "I promise."

"Better than our best," Sophie added.

He smiled and pointed the stem of his pipe at her.

"Don't promise too much now," he said. "I'll see the two of you tomorrow. Come by the front door, but I'll have keys made up for the greenhouse so that you'll be able to come and go as you like from your studio."

We stood there for a long moment after he was gone.

"Did that just happen?" Sophie asked finally.

"I think so. Perhaps we're dreaming—ow! Why'd you pinch me?"

"Just making sure."

I poked her in the stomach with a stiff finger and she tried to look fierce as she planned her revenge, but then we both dissolved into laughter.

"Why do you think he's doing this?" I asked when we'd recovered.

"You heard him. He thinks we have potential. You, I can see, of course, but—"

"Oh, don't be so modest," I told her. "You have talent dripping from your fingers."

She gave her hand a curious look, then danced back as I tried to poke her again.

"But it's just that, right?" I said. "He's not…you know..?"

Sophie shook her head. "I've never heard of him chasing after students. Not like that creepy Professor Miller."

I pulled a face.

"And he's quite brilliant," Sophie went on. "Not just with art history."

I nodded. "Wendy was telling me. He's written all these books on mythology and folk stories and stuff."

"I've read a couple. They're a bit dry, but really interesting."

"So you think it's on the level?"

"There's only one way to find out. Don't forget to bring your fierce Tyson girl side."

"I wish. I was never fierce."

"Fiercer than me."

It was on the level. It was amazing. We had this huge greenhouse with amazing light during the day. At night there were all these natural lights that people would normally use for growing plants. It was warm and cozy. Yes, there were geraniums and bulbs being stored, lending the area a wonderful, earthy smell—until we killed that with our turps. They were kept in a smaller section to one side, which was glassed off from the area we made into our studio.

Goon was as cranky as the professor had warned us—and odd looking, too. A round ball of a little man, with spindly arms and legs, and a wide face with a pair of slightly slanted eyes that could glare enough to make you shiver in your shoes. But we got used to him, and the glare, and were soon paying neither any more mind that you might to a bad-tempered dog always barking at you when you walked by his yard.

We spent all our free time there, painting and drawing, studying and writing essays. It became the hangout for the little family we'd made for ourselves: Sophie and I, Wendy, her friend Mona, Geordie, Angel and Lou, and even Geordie's brother Christy. I say "even" because Christy and Geordie didn't get along a lot of the time and were forever sniping at each other. Alone, each of them was a delight.

I liked Christy, but I tended to take Geordie's side in any disagreement between the two because, well, after all, I'd met him first.

It was strange that they could be at odds with each other as often as they were because they were so much alike. Neither attended university—Geordie hadn't even finished high school—but they were dedicated and self-taught, each determined to make a living through their art: Geordie's music and Christy's writing.

Christy and I got along well when it was just the two of us because he loved to ramble on about magical things and beings—most of what he wrote was about them, odd occurrences, ghost stories, urban legends—and I loved to hear about that kind of thing. I didn't believe in fairies and hobgoblins and all the things he talked about, but the difference between most people and me was that I *wanted* to believe they were real.

The professor turned out to be a perfect gentleman and exactly what he'd made himself out to be: a patron of the arts. We were forever coming into the studio to find a package of pencils, some new sketchbooks, tubes of paint and the like that he'd left for us with a small note saying that he'd found these while rummaging in a drawer, or in the basement, and thought we could use them more than he.

We weren't fooled, any more than we had been by the two brand new easels that were waiting for us that first afternoon. We tried to protest at first, and give things back to him, but he'd get such a hurt look that we'd end up having to keep them. And we certainly needed these extra supplies because, as it was, both Sophie and I were forever scrounging to make ends meet.

Sometimes the professor would drop by when our friends were over and he ended up fitting easily into our little gatherings. The day he realized that Christy shared the same interests in folklore and local myth that he did, we ended up losing the older Riddell brother. When he came over after that, more often than not, he'd go straight to the professor's library where the pair of them would spend hours talking, arguing, discussing. They were like little boys with baseball cards, talking about their dream teams, except their conversations revolved around fairy tales and *genii loci* and the strange creatures that were supposed to live in Newford's subway tunnels and sewer system.

Sometimes Geordie would play music for us while we worked—either on his fiddle, or these albums he'd picked up on his endless trawls through the thrift shops. The professor had given us an old record player he wasn't using anymore—and this time it really was something that had to have been banging around in the house for ages. But battered though it was, and even if we sometimes had to tape a dime to the arm to keep the needle from skittering across the vinyl, it filled the greenhouse with music.

Music. That was one of Geordie's big gifts to me.

The Carters didn't care for music. We didn't have a record player, or even a radio, when I was growing up. And then later, when I was living on the street, I had more pressing concerns than music, though

I did hear some. But music's not the same when you're high. I never did psychedelics, so maybe it's different with them. But when you're on some cocktail of speed and the brown, just trying to find oblivion for as long as you can hold onto it, music's a distraction, even an irritation.

Geordie showed me the other side, cherrypicking the albums so that I was introduced to the best music without having to wade through the less-inspiring stuff to get to the gold.

There were the songs and dance tunes of Ireland and Scotland, of course, they being Geordie's first love. Flute players and fiddlers. Harpists, pipers and box players. Margaret Barry and the Dubliners and Seán Ó Riada. Na Filí and the Exiles and the Chieftains—which I thought was Indian music at first, from the band's name, much to Geordie's amusement.

From the first, I loved this music as much as Geordie did. It was the soundtrack to the fairy tales I'd so loved growing up. I'd hear Séamus Ennis' uillean pipes, or John Doherty on fiddle, and in my mind I was walking through a glorious landscape of once-upon-a-times.

But it wasn't just Celtic music that Geordie introduced me to. There was so much I hadn't known.

Dylan and Leonard Cohen and Tim Hardin. The Beatles and the Incredible String Band and all those fun girl groups like the Shangri-las. Mahler and Brahms, Mozart and those gorgeous violin concertos by Paganini. Traditional South American music and Spanish fandango. There was never an end to the fantastic music Geordie brought over, like a magician pulling an endless scarf out of his sleeve.

I learned so much from him. I learned so much from everybody.

Wendy would often sit quietly in a corner working on her poetry, or studying, but she could talk for hours about the Beat poets, Charles Bukowski, or Walt Whitman. It was because of her that I began my lifetime love affair with the works of Gary Snyder.

Mona would draw cartoons—many of which we insisted stay in the studio, tacked to the bulletin board that we'd fastened to the wall beside the door that led into the house. She introduced me to the whole underground comic scene—all these mimeographed booklets that she and her friends produced which were about things we could understand and relate to because they mirrored our own lives.

We gave our studio a name, the way that famous artists' studios often had names. Ours we named The Grumbling Greenhouse Studio in honour of Goon, though we never called it that when he was around.

But while sometimes we had a real crowd, mostly it was just Sophie and me, there in the studio. At night, with the overhead lights pushing the darkness of the garden at bay. Painting. Working out proportions in our sketchbooks. Doing colour studies before we put expensive paint on expensive canvasses.

Sometimes we wouldn't say a word to each other for hours. There'd be only the sound of a pencil on paper. A brush on canvass. Pages turning in one of our school books.

But sometimes we'd just sit side by side on the old sofa the professor had Goon bring out for us. We'd sit there and talk for hours. About nothing and everything.

"If you had the chance," Sophie asked one night while we sat there, fresh tea in our mugs, our brushes soaking in turpentine, "would you go back in time and change things?"

I knew exactly what she was talking about and "yes" was the first thing that came to mind. Absolutely. In a minute.

But before I actually said the word, I thought about my family. The Carters. Uneducated, and proud of it. Losers, except there was always somebody else to blame. It was never their fault. No Carter would ever amount to much of anything. But here I was, actually attending university. Living in the city. Making friends, working, helping other people. In other words, turning into a normal person.

What would have happened if I hadn't gone through hell first?

Would I have turned into my mother? Old before her time, bitter, with five kids that she didn't love, and a husband she liked even less.

I'm not saying I appreciated what I'd had to go through, or that I should be grateful. But if I hadn't, I'd be a different person, wouldn't I?

Would I want to be that person, now that I was finally becoming somebody I could actually like?

"I don't know," I said. "If I could go back, maybe it would only be to tell the little girl I was that it'll get better."

Sophie nodded. "Yeah, I don't know either. On the one hand, if I could have stopped my mother…or even got to ask her *why* she was leaving us…maybe that would have been better. But maybe it would only have made things worse. And if I hadn't gone through what I did—"

"You wouldn't be the person you are now."

She smiled. "Something like that. Stupid, really."

"I don't think so."

Sophie had a sip of her tea. On the other side of the greenhouse windows, I could hear the wind rattling a loose shutter and was surprised that Goon hadn't seen to it before the shutter had even decided to start rattling.

"What are you most scared of?" Sophie asked.

I turned to look at her.

"That all that crap will happen to me again," I said without having to think about it. "What I had to go through as a kid, and then after. That need for the dead zone of heroin just to get through the day, the hour, the minute."

Sophie shook her head. "You wouldn't let that happen."

"No, but I'm scared of it all the same."

"I'm scared of the people I love now leaving me the way my mother left my dad and me."

I nodded. I could see that. And while I couldn't fix my own fears, I could maybe help with hers. At least insofar as I was concerned.

"I won't do that," I told her. "I'd never do that to you."

"Promise me," she said. "Promise me that you'll talk to me first. That you'll tell me where and why you're going."

"I promise," I told her.

And I meant it.

Except I hadn't, had I? Offered the easy route to all the things I wanted, I'd done to her *exactly* what her mother had.

-9-

I don't know how long I'm kneeling there beside the canal. I've cried so much, I'm utterly exhausted. It reminds me of those endless days and nights in the Chelsea Arms, knowing I'll never get over the need, the pain, the burning ache. Knowing I was less than nothing and no matter how hard I tried, I'd never be anything but the miserable excuse of a waste of space that I was.

I managed to get past that—and all the horrible doubts and fears that kept returning—but it was only through the love and support of my friends. And how had I repaid them?

I know what I have to do.

I push myself slowly to my feet and stagger away from the canal, the whispers pulling at me, trying to hold me back. But whether I stay or go, it doesn't really matter. Distance doesn't really matter. The whispers stay in my head and now I know just what Cholo's friend Petey had been going through that first night I'd met them on the basketball court. All those awful things I'd been hearing by the canal—they were on an endless loop inside my head that I couldn't stop.

Except maybe with a fix.

Just enough to get the damned whispers to shut up for a moment and let me think.

To let me do what I needed to do.

I lean against the side of a building, half a block away from the canal, and press my cheek against the rough stone.

I know dope's not the answer.

I know it'll just make things worse.

But I can't stop thinking of the long cool oblivion that a hit would let me fall into.

I push away from the building and go on, shuffling my feet, one foot in front of the other, the whispers accompanying me every step of the way.

It takes me a long time to get back to Donna and Tommy's apartment building.

When I'm inside the foyer and start up the stairs, all I want to do is go to my own place and sprawl out on the bed. I want to lie there and press my face into the pillow and pray for sleep. Because I'm exhausted. I'm so wrung out I can barely keep my head up. The whispers press and press and press at me. I keep wanting to cry but there's nothing left inside.

My apartment's not far—just down the hall. I could go and lie down, just for a few minutes. Just until the looping whispers quiet down.

I almost do it, too, but I only let myself pause at my landing and sit down on a riser to collect myself.

Except I can't think.

Shut up, I tell the whispers. I'm doing it. I'm going to go back. So just shut up.

Shut. The. Fuck. Up.

I don't realize I said the words aloud until I hear a door open on the landing above mine. I lift my head at the sound of bare feet padding down the hall. A moment later, Donna's at the top of the stairs, looking down at me.

"J.C.?" she says. "Are you okay?"

I shake my head.

"What's the matter?"

"Everything."

I find that if I squeeze my hands really tightly, fingernails digging into my palms, the pain keeps the whispers enough at bay for me to talk. Donna comes down the stairs and sits beside me.

"Yeah, you don't look so good," she says. "What happened?"

I turn to look at her.

"I *went* to the canal," I tell her. "I heard them."

She doesn't have to ask. I guess everybody here knows about the whispers. She only gives a slow nod.

"The whispers," she says.

"Yeah."

"You know they don't tell the truth."

I shake my head. "Cholo says they exaggerate what people are really saying about you, but they're still based on something real."

"Who the hell is Cholo?"

"Just this guy. It doesn't matter. All I know is that I can't stay here."

"You can't mean that."

I dig my nails into my palms a little harder.

"Can't you see why I have to go back?" I ask.

"Honestly, no. This is the perfect life. What does it matter how you get it?"

"It matters," I tell her. "You have no idea what I went through to get clean. I went through hell."

"C'mon, J.C. Sure, I—"

"No, you don't. You just died and came here and reinvented yourself. I had to fight for everything I gained."

"That's a little, harsh."

"Maybe. But am I wrong?"

"No. I don't know. Maybe. I didn't choose for things to work out the way they did."

"But you expect me to choose this place and stay here with you. To throw away everything I earned and now just take the easy ride. To let the people who helped me—who believed in me—think I just took off. Went on some crazy bender and disappeared back into the sewer that they pulled me out of."

"J.C., you—"

"I *heard* them talking…all my friends…"

"Okay," she says. "It was always your decision to make. If you want to change your mind, you can. I'll take you back to the club tomorrow."

When she says that, the pressure in my head eases off a little. The whispers have become an old heartache now. I can still hear them, but their endless looping refrain has quieted enough to be bearable.

"Thanks," I say.

Donna shrugs. We sit there quietly for awhile and I remember all those times back in the Home for Wayward Girls when we'd do this, just sit together, not needing to talk. I feel a different kind of heart-ache then.

"I'm going to miss you," I tell her. "I always thought we'd get together again, you know, back home..."

She nods. "I'll miss you, too."

It's quiet again, then. I look at my palms, each of them marked with four welts in the shape of quarter moons.

"Remember what I told you," she says after a few moments. "If you return to Newford, it's a one-way trip. You can't come back here."

"I remember."

"And..."

I wait, but she doesn't go on.

"And what?" I finally ask.

"You won't remember being here. When you're back in the world of the living, you'll forget everything from when you walked through the door of Cool Hand's Juke. It'll be like it never happened."

I shake my head. "No. I only forget the things I want to forget."

"You're not going to have a choice."

"I'll forget *you*?"

"Not that we once knew each other," she says. "But you'll forget that you saw me again. That we had...you know, this extra time together."

"So it's all or nothing."

"I don't make the rules, J.C. I just have to play by them like everybody else."

I sigh. And then something else occurs to me.

"My friends all think I've gone on a binge somewhere," I say, "but I won't be able to tell them different, will I? God, how am I supposed to face them?"

"I'm sorry. I never wanted it to work out this way. I really thought you'd be happy here."

"I was. I am. But it doesn't feel real."

"It is real—just a different kind of real."

"I suppose. I guess I wish I could have both worlds. Or at least you and the new friends I've made here along with my new life back home."

She doesn't say anything. What can she say? But I feel like I need to explain it more. Or better.

"It's not just people," I say. "Back there…I feel I can make a difference."

"You can do the same thing here."

I shake my head. "No, I can't. Here, everything just works out for everybody, and that's cool. That's great. But that's going to happen whether I'm here or not."

"You can't solve all the world's problems."

"No. But I can work on solving the ones around me. And even if I just bring a little hope into somebody else's life…you know, working in a soup kitchen, or sitting with someone in a hospice, or an old folk's home. That's something. That's something I can do that means something."

"And staying here won't."

She doesn't make a question of it and all I can do is repeat what I told her earlier.

"I'll miss you, Donna," I say.

She takes my head and gives it a squeeze.

She takes me back to Cool Hand's Juke the next morning.

The neighbourhood's very different by day, the streets full of vehicles, the sidewalks crowded. Almost every street corner has little carts selling coffee or pretzels or hot dogs and the real estate along the shop fronts is taken up with people selling every sort of thing you can imagine from little tables and blankets. Jewelry, crafts, books and records, handmade clothing, art.

Ti'Jean, the big doorman, is still on the door, though the club's not open. He's sitting in a chair reading a paper, but he smiles when he looks up to see us approach. The smile fades when Donna tells him why we were here.

"You know how it works," he says. "You come in one door, you go out another."

My heart sinks as he says that and I remember Cholo telling me the same thing. I'd just forgotten.

But Donna obviously had never heard this before. She shakes her head.

"I *don't* know how it works," she says. "Who makes up all these stupid rules, anyway?"

"Nobody makes them up. It's just the way things are."

"But how does Jilly get back? I promised her she could. That it was her choice if she stays or goes back."

Ti'Jean studies me for a moment.

"Looks like she's already made the choice to stay," he says.

"No, I haven't," I tell him. "I was still just thinking about it. Now I've made up my mind. I want to go home."

"Then why don't you have that glow of the living still clinging to you?" he asks. "I'll admit you've got some kind of glow coming out of you, but it's something different."

Again with the light, aura, whatever.

"Please, Ti'Jean," Donna says.

He shakes his head. "It's not that I don't want to help you. It's that I can't. We only get the one free ride, and it's a long time until the next Halloween."

"What does that mean?" I ask.

"The dead can come back that day," Donna explains. "We can manifest in the world of the living, appearing at the place we died. It's how I was able to see you to invite you to the club."

"I forgot about that. So your band doesn't really play at stock car races and hot rod shows like you said, does it?"

"No, we do. They're just here—in this world."

I nod. Then something else occurs to me.

"I thought you said you died in jail?"

She shook her head. "I died in an ambulance on the way to the hospital. When I reappear in your world, it's at the corner of Norton and Flood where the ambulance was waiting at a light. When I went back, I just had to hope the traffic was light or I would have gotten whacked by some car before I could get out of the street." She turns back to Ti'Jean. "If you can't help us, do you know anyone who can?"

"I don't know. Maybe someone in one of those little joints on Jordan Street."

"Thanks. We'll try that."

Ti'Jean puts one of those big hands of his on my arm and gives me an awkward pat.

"I'm sorry," he says. "If I could help, I would."

"I know," I tell him. "It's okay."

Though it's not really. While we've been talking, when it becomes clear I'm not going to just be able to step back into my own world, the whispers have started to get a little louder. They're not incapacitating. At least not yet. I don't know what I'll do if they come back full force like they were last night.

"C'mon," Donna says. "Jordan Street's near where I took you that first morning. We didn't get to it, but it's full of these teahouses and mystery shops with all kinds of fortune tellers and herbalists and people like that."

We say our goodbyes to Ti'Jean and she leads me off to the bus stop.

"Mystery shops?" I ask.

She shrugs. "You know. Places were they sell stuff and you have no idea what it is or what it's for."

"This seems kind of a funny city for a fortune teller," I say. "Considering everybody here's already dead so they know how their lives turn out."

"I guess. But there is another place after this one."

"You mean you die again?"

She shakes her head. "Not exactly. You just kind of go on. I don't really know. I've only heard about it."

"Well, I guess we can find out on Jordan Street," I say.

The streets around Cool Hand's Juke seemed lively, but Jordan Street runs through an area that Donna calls Cobbletown—it's an old part of the city with narrower streets and cobblestoned streets which reminds me of the Lee Street Market back in Newford. It's bustling with street vendors and dozens of curious little shops and boutiques, selling everything from beads and bangles to Chinese herbal remedies. There are junk shops, book shops, used record stores, thrift shops. There are designer clothing stores, art galleries, coffee shops and teahouses. Farmers' produce sold from the back of pickup trucks side by side with rickety tables laden with colourful rugs from India and the Middle East.

There are people everywhere and it feels like a carnival.

At either end of Jordan Street, which is only a block long, there's a small town square with tents and stalls set up under the tall oak trees. In the corner of the square near our bus stop a troupe of actors is putting on a play and I think of Rebecca Rebecca and her improvateers. I smile until I see a fiddler among the various buskers on the sidewalks across from the square and the whisper in my head calls up Geordie's voice.

Shut up, shut up, I think, but paying any kind of attention to it only makes it louder.

I lift my hand and squeeze my temples with my thumb and ring finger.

"Do you have a headache?" Donna asks.

"No."

I don't want to talk about it.

"Where do we start?" I ask her.

"I haven't a clue. I guess we'll just try asking somebody."

Before I can say something about how maybe we should be a bit more methodical than that, she's already walking up to the old man selling newspapers beside a coffee cart a few yards up from the bus stop. I look at the headlines of his papers while they talk. I haven't looked at a newspaper since I got here—it's not a habit I've ever gotten into because who needs more bad news? But apparently you don't get bad news here. Today's main story is about some marathon that happened yesterday with a big picture of the winner. The other stories on the front page are about a pedigreed boxer who came in first at a dog show and a woman who makes beautiful hat boxes out of cardboard she finds in the trash.

I find myself getting annoyed looking at the paper, and wonder why that is. Isn't this what any sane person would want? A better world without war, or crime, or poverty, or illness?

Except it's not real. That's the problem. It's a playground for the dead, and while it may be real for them, it's not for the few hapless people like myself who are stupid enough to get stuck here.

I make myself tune into the conversation Donna's having. The newspaper vendor has a lead for her—he thinks someone named Julianna will be able to help us—but he doesn't know where to find her.

"Ask at the Willow Withy," he says. He point down Jordan Street. "It's a teahouse about halfway down the block. Someone there will know where she is."

Except they don't, we find out after we thank the newspaper vendor and ask at the teahouse. The waitress there sends us to a curio shop down a little alley and the woman there directs us to a vintage clothing store the next block over. The woman there says she saw this Julianna an hour or so ago and that we should try the farmers' market.

"This is hopeless," I say.

The woman in the clothing shop told us to circle back to the square on this side of Jordan and aim for the area of tents and pickup trucks.

"You can't miss Julianna," she told us. "Just look for a tall, beautiful woman with a waterfall of red hair."

It's almost noon and there are a million people milling about the sidewalks and square. Okay, I'm exaggerating, but there are a lot of people, talking and laughing and wandering about, and once it's filtered through my ears, every sound they make seems to translate into the whispers I heard in the canal last night, and they just keep getting louder. The barrage of sound inside my head is making it almost impossible to think.

I squeeze my temples again and Donna gives me a worried look.

I so need something to make the looping words shut up. Something to dull my brain. At this point I'd happily succumb to anything. A joint would be good. A spoon of the brown better. I'd settle for a couple of shots of tequila or whiskey.

"Tall. Red-haired," I say, repeating what the woman in the clothing shop told us as I try to concentrate.

If we find her and she can't help, maybe she'll be able to hook me up with a dealer, because I'm going to need *something* if these whispers don't shut up soon.

"There," Donna says, pointing into the crowd. "I think I see her."

I don't know if I'm going to last long enough to even be able to explain my problem. But I follow in Donna's wake and finally see the woman we're looking for. At least I see a tall, gorgeous woman with a wild mane of red hair, getting apples from the back of a truck. We get up beside her and wait for her to finish her conversation with the vendor.

"Excuse me," Donna says when the woman turns away from the vendor with her bag of apples. "We were told you might be able to help us."

The woman looks at her, then her deep blue gaze turns to me.

"Oh, you poor thing," she says.

She reaches out with her free and lays her palm on top of my head. I'm startled, and my need for personal space—especially when it comes to strangers—kicks in. But before I can jerk away from her hand, I feel something…it's impossible to describe. It's like a long, cool shock. It starts at the top of my head where her hand lies and instantly spreads through my entire body. And just like that, the voices in my head fall silent.

She lifts her hand away and I shake my head. The sudden inner silence makes me feel as though my ears are blocked. For a long moment I'm wrapped in a cocoon of utter silence, then the noise of the people and the traffic comes trickling back to me. And it's just that. Everyday noise like you'd hear in any city. The looping whispers don't start up inside my head again.

"I'm afraid the relief you're feeling is only temporary," the woman says. "Why don't we find a quiet place and you can tell me how those horrible gossips came to get such a powerful grip on you."

"Gossips?" I say.

She shrugs. "Gossips, whispers. Whatever you want to call them."

"I'd just like to get rid of them."

"Can you do that?" Donna asks.

She doesn't know how absolutely pit-low I was feeling, but she sees that whatever the woman did has helped me.

"I can't tell until I know the whole story," the woman says. "I'm Julianna, by the way. And how on earth did you find me? I've been everywhere this morning."

Donna introduces us, then adds, "We've just been asking around."

"Well, I could do with a bit of quiet," she says, then looks at me and adds, "and I'm sure you'd appreciate it."

"The crowds doesn't bother me at all," I tell her, "not now that you've stopped the noise in my head. How did you do that?"

"It won't last," she says, which isn't an answer at all, and fills me with the dreadful anticipation of the whispers return. "Come along."

She leads us out of the square and down another one of the cobblestoned streets, then ducks into what I think is an alleyway at first, but as we step under an archway thick with vines, I realize it's the entrance to a courtyard. The yard is cobbletoned as well, but there are a half-dozen small tables set out with checkered cloths and wine bottles holding candles. There's greenery everywhere, growing out of planters and windowboxes.

I suppose this is some sort of café or restaurant, although there's no one sitting at the tables. But as soon as we step into the courtyard, a small, dark-haired man comes out of one the many doors that lead off from the open area, smiling from ear to ear—I mean literally. He's got the widest mouth I've ever seen. And his dark eyes, though certainly friendly, don't seem to have any whites. It's as though they're all iris.

He wipes his hands on a cotton apron, then ushers us to a table.

"Welcome, welcome," he says. "It's always such a pleasure to see you, Madame Julianna." He includes us, by adding, "And of course, any friend of yours, is our honoured guest as well."

Julianna seems amused by the effusive greeting, but she also takes it in stride, as though it's her due.

"Thank you, Nasir," she says. "Would you bring us some tea—the blue flower blend, please. And we don't need menus, unless..?"

She turns to us, eyebrows raised.

"No, we're good," Donna says.

I nod. "Tea would be great. I don't need anything else."

Nasir takes the time to hold our chairs for us—Julianna's first, of course—then hurries back inside. He's obviously in awe of her. And thinking about it, everyone we passed on the way here, seemed to hold a certain deference towards her.

"Who *are* you?" Donna says, which tells me she noticed the same thing.

Julianna smiles and sets her bag on the cobblestones by her chair.

"You came looking for me," she says. "I would think that you would already know the answer to that question."

We both shake our heads.

"Well, contrary to Nasir's effusive welcome," she says, "I'm no one special. But I do have somewhat of a reputation of being a…I suppose one might call it a conjurer."

"You mean like you can do magic?" Donna says.

I'm not surprised. After whatever she did with the laying on of hands bit earlier, not only are the whispers gone, but I'm feeling really grounded and safe. I certainly don't feel the need for a fix anymore—unless what she did to me was the magical equivalent.

"Why are you so surprised?" Julianna asks Donna. "Isn't that why you sought me out?"

"I…" Donna looks at me for a moment before returning her attention to Julianna. "I guess we were looking for something. I just didn't think of it as magic, but that'd work. Though I have to say it's not something I ever thought of as real."

"And yet you live here, after your death elsewhere?"

"Yeah, but…"

Her voice trails off and Nasir returns at that moment, bearing a tray with three porcelain mugs and a big clay teapot that gives off an enticing, if entirely unfamiliar, aroma. With an elaborate flourish, he pours us each a mug, Julianna first, again. She takes a sip, then smiles at him.

"Perfect."

He beams, nods to Donna and me, then hurries off once more.

"Blue flower tea," Donna says, doubt in her voice. "What kind of blue flower?"

But I trust Julianna. If she could fix the noise in my head with just the touch of her hand, why would she be offering us something that wasn't good for us?

I blow at the steam of my own mug, then take a sip. It doesn't taste like anything I've ever had before, but at the same time, it seems to hold the best of everything I've ever liked in it. It's spicy and aromatic with just a wee touch of sweetness.

"It's absolutely delicious," I say.

Donna finally tries hers and she smiles with her whole face.

"It's a special tea that Nasir keeps for me," Julianna tells us. "The name's a bit of a misnomer, since I use every part of the plant to make it."

"Where do these flowers grow?" Donna asks.

Julianna smiles. "Not in this world. Now tell me," she adds, turning to me, "How can I help you? I know you're being plagued by the worst case of whispers I've ever seen. Back at the farmer's market, I could hear them before I even turned to look at you."

"You can read minds?" I find myself saying.

"Hardly. If I could, I wouldn't need to ask you this, would I?"

"No, I guess not."

I tell her the whole story, from meeting Donna, to finding out from Ti'Jean this morning that I can't go back. I just give her the high points version. I figure there's no need to tell her every single detail or piece of conversation. Donna adds a bit here, a bit there, but mostly she lets me tell the story my own way.

Julianna studies me the whole time I talk.

"I have to get back," I say, finishing. "I don't belong here."

"I agree," she says. "It was unfortunate happenstance that put you in this situation. But I'm afraid I can't help you."

"Don't tells us that," Donna says. "We could pay you or, you know, work out a trade or something."

Julianna shakes her head. "It's not that. If I could help you, I would so without expecting recompense. I partake of nothing here that I haven't brought myself. Not food, not drink, not favours. Elsewise I would be in the same unhappy circumstances that Jilly is."

I think of fairy tales, how you're not supposed to eat or drink in them, because then you're stuck in fairyland forever, and I guess it makes a horrible kind of sense.

"Why can't you help me?" I ask.

I shiver in anticipation, waiting for the whispers to start up again. But so far they're leaving me alone. Maybe it's the lingering effect of

Julianna's laying on of hands earlier. Maybe it's her blue flower tea. Maybe it's just her, sitting there across the little checker-clothed table from me, her blue eyes unhappy with what she's telling me.

"You can't go back," she says. "Not after accepting Mireya's bounty."

"I don't know what you mean. Who's Mireya?"

She gave a lazy wave of her arm. "Here. This city. Everything around us."

"So the city's called Mireya."

I look at Donna. She only shrugs to say she's never heard the name before. But Julianna nods.

"As is the spirit whose domain this is," she says. "The one whose bounty you accepted."

"I never accepted anything from any spirit."

"Do you have a place to live?"

"Yes, but—"

"Do you have a source of income?"

"Well, if you can call it that. Like I said, somebody I never heard of made all these investments for me and—"

She cuts me off by opening her hands in front of her in a "there you have it" gesture.

"That is Mireya's bounty. Given to you by her. Accepted by you from her. The bargain has been made and kept."

"That's not fair. I didn't know what I was doing."

I hear how stupid that sounds even as I'm saying it. Yes, it's not fair, but that's the way of the world. Just because you don't know the rules, doesn't mean they're not there. But it turns out that it really is like fairyland here, and all those stories of not drinking or eating when you're in the fairies' court are true. Julianna's no dummy. Why else was she so emphatic about not even accepting a favour here?

"That's why you don't eat or drink the food here," I say.

She lifts her tea mug. "Unless I bring it myself."

"Then why were you buying apples?" Donna asks.

"I wasn't. I'm only running an errand for a friend."

"So, basically, I'm screwed," I say, bringing us back to the real matter at hand.

I say the words, but they're not really sinking in. I was so sure that Julianna would be able to help me.

She gives a slow nod of her head, those blue eyes of hers filled with compassion.

"You have to stay here, yes," she says.

"And my friends are never going to know what happened to me."

Oh, Sophie, I think. I'm so sorry.

Because that's the worst of it. I'll miss all of them, but I know how much this is going to hurt Sophie. When the whispers take her voice, it hurts the most, because I'd *promised* her…

"If that's your most pressing concern…" Julianna begins.

I lean forward.

"Tell me," I say when she doesn't go on. "*Is* there something you can do?"

"I can send a piece of you back," she says. "To all intents and purposes it will be you."

I have no idea what she's talking about.

"A piece of me..?"

She nods. "You could call it your shadow—all the parts of you that you don't want. It's possible to split it off from who you consider yourself to be. You will have to stay here, but it would be able to return because it hasn't made a bargain with Mireya the way you have."

"I don't understand. When you say you'd make it out of all the parts of me that I don't want, does that mean it'll be some horrible version of myself?"

"As it experiences life, it will grow and change the same as you have. But at the start, yes. It will be all the parts of yourself that you reject when you consider who you are."

This is starting to ring a bell. I can remember Christy and the professor talking about this one evening.

All the parts of me that I don't want. So my shadow will be some poor junkie victim with a history of abuse?

"And then what happens to her?" I ask. "This shadow version of me?"

"She lives your life. It would be longer than yours—supernatural beings tend to have longer life spans—but eventually she will die."

"And come here."

"Not necessarily. There are many places the dead can go."

I know from the evasive look in her eyes that she's not telling me everything. Growing up the way I did, you quickly learn when people aren't sharing the whole truth with you.

"But what?" I ask.

"There's no but."

I don't say anything. I just hold her gaze until she sighs and looks away. When she looks back I see something I can't read in her eyes.

"There are those who argue that shadows don't have a soul," she finally says.

"So, I'd be okaying the creation of some messed-up and weaker version of myself who doesn't have a soul?"

"I don't *know*."

But then I get it.

"Except it doesn't have to be that way, does it?" Donna says. "This shadow girl can change and make something of herself if she wants to, right? You could tell her the things she should and shouldn't do, if she wants a better life.

Julianna shakes her head. "No, Jilly will be here and the shadow—when she's created—will be there."

She doesn't look at Donna while she speaks. She holds my gaze and she sees that I know.

"That's what you are, aren't you?" I say. "Or at least it's how you started out."

She nods. "It's why I can walk between the worlds. It's why I don't need to be bound to any one place, or accept any guardian spirit's bounty. It's why I'm so self-sufficient."

Donna's looking back and forth between us in confusion.

"Wait a sec'," she says. "What did I miss here?"

"How can you think you don't have a soul?" I say to Julianna.

"I don't know one way or another."

"But nobody knows for certain. I mean, not absolutely, scientifically, here's the proof."

"Except," Donna says, "all the people being here make a pretty good argument that we do."

We both look at her.

"She's right," I say.

"For those born human," Julianna allows.

"You look perfectly normal to me."

She nods. "And so will your shadow, living your life that will become hers. But she'll have no more had a natural birth than I ever did."

"You don't think I should do it, do you?"

"It's not my decision to make."

"Yeah, I get that."

I fall silent for a long moment. I look across the courtyard and follow the antics of a sparrow who keeps hopping down for crumbs on the cobblestones under a table, then flying nervously away to the tallest branches of a shrub in one of the planters. There's a tabby cat in the window nearby and the bird can't be sure that it won't somehow get out and eat her.

I can feel Donna and Julianna looking at me, waiting for me to make up my mind. But I don't have to. I've already made it up. I'm just holding off telling them because it feels like as long as I do, the longer everything can just stay the same. My friends back in the other world still won't know what's happened to me, but at least I don't have the whispers banging around in my head, trying to drive me insane.

But I know the moment can't last. Moments never do. One follows the other, just like trying to clean up your messes follows your having made the mistakes in the first place. I watch the sparrow make another nervous foray down for the crumbs, then turn back to look at Julianna.

"I can't do it," I say. "I don't know how it'd turn out for this shadow of mine, but while I can deal with screwing up my own life, I'm not going to take the chance I'll do it to someone else."

Like I already have to Sophie.

Julianna leans forward. "You're sure?"

"I'm sure. I'm just going to have to think of some other way to fix this."

I'm expecting Donna to pipe up, but whatever she's thinking, she's keeping it to herself.

Julianna runs a hand through her long red hair, then settles back in her chair.

"You are a contradiction," she says, "but I can see why Mireya would want to keep you."

"What do you mean?"

"You wear a face of worry and fear, but under it you carry a great and golden light that would burn away all your uncertainties, if only you would let it."

Again, with the light. But it makes me think of Sophie, and that makes the hollow place inside me all that more desolate. I wish I really did have some wonderful light that could do what Julianna says. Maybe then I wouldn't keep screwing up all the time.

"But as it is," Julianna goes on, "that potential stays here in the city and helps to sustain her."

"I don't understand."

I don't think I've said that, or "What do you mean?", more often than I have in the past few days.

"The guardian spirits like Mireya are generous in their largess," she explains. "But it's the bargains they make with those who accept their bounty that keeps them prosperous enough to be able to do so. I have been to other cities that are broken and desolate, their guardian spirits almost entirely dispersed, because they were forgotten or ignored."

I remember what Gus, the cranky old man I met in the park told me about how there are all kinds of different worlds in the afterlife, this place—what he called the City of the Unfulfilled Dead—being only one of them. I guess he wasn't so far off the mark after all. And even when it came to the whispers…he was right about them, too. He told me they'd tell me the truth. He just didn't tell me how much it would hurt.

Maybe I should have another talk with him. Maybe he'll have a solution for me, though no doubt it will be painful and hard.

"Let me know what you decide," Julianna says.

"I'm pretty sure I won't change my mind," I tell her.

"But just saying we do," Donna adds, finally speaking up. "How will we find you again?"

"I know you now. You have only to speak my name and I can come to you."

"Because you're a shadow," I say.

She shakes her head. "No, because I am a conjurer."

She leans down and picks up the bag of apples by her feet.

"I will come to you," she says, "as easily as I leave you now."

And with that last word still hanging in the air, Donna and I are staring at an empty chair.

"Holy crap," Donna says. She turns to look around our table. "How did she do that?"

"Magic," I say in a small voice.

It's funny. I'm here in a city peopled by the dead of my own world, but somehow that doesn't seem nearly as astonishing as having Julianna just disappear from her chair. I suppose it's because the city, for all its own magical origin, still seems pretty normal.

Except for the whispers.

And the funny thing about no one being around much once the evening gets late.

"So let's sum it up," Donna says. "You can't go back home, but your shadow can."

"Except it wouldn't be me."

She nods. "Do you think she can really do this?"

"She disappeared, didn't she?"

"Right. She sure did." Donna waits a beat, then goes. "But you don't want to do it."

"I can't. I know what the shadow would be and I won't do that to her."

"It seems to have worked out pretty well for Julianna," she says, "being all respected and magicky."

"And unhappy," I say.

"I didn't get that."

"Maybe you just weren't looking for it."

I stand up from the table and look around. The sparrow's gone now, but the cat's still in the window. I turn to the door the waiter's been using.

"I wonder if we're supposed to pay that Nasir guy," I say.

"I don't think so," Donna says. "We were drinking Julianna's tea."

"I guess."

She stand up as well and gives me a concerned look.

"How's your head?" she asks.

She means the whispers.

"It's still quiet."

Neither of us say anything about hoping the quiet will last. We both know it won't.

"So what do we do now?" Donna asks. "Do you want to go back to the apartment?"

"You go ahead," I tell her. "I need to walk around a bit and try to figure this all out."

"Don't..." she starts to say, but she doesn't finish.

I know she meant well, but what could she say? Don't worry too much? Don't listen to the whispers? Don't drive yourself crazy?

"Just, you know, take care," she says.

"I will."

We walk together under the ivy-hung archway and down the short alley. When we reach the street, I take her arm and pull her into a hug.

"I'm so sorry," she says. "I thought I was doing a good thing."

"I know," I tell her. "And I love you for it."

Then she goes one way and I go the other.

Where am I going? I'm not really sure. Maybe to look for Gus. Or maybe just to appreciate the quiet in my head while it lasts.

-10-

Angel had been busy with a custody case, spending long days in court, and I hadn't seen much of her over the past week. We'd talked on the phone, but it wasn't the same, so this morning we'd made a date to have breakfast at the Dear Mouse Diner on Lee Street, just the two of us. I had a class in an hour, and she had a meeting with her client's lawyer, but at the moment we didn't have to think about anything except our breakfast and each other's company.

On the table between us, we each had one mug of the only addiction I now allowed myself: hot steaming coffee, freshly brewed behind the Dear Mouse's long Formica counter. Other than that, Angel was being good with a bowl of granola and a glass of orange juice, while I had bacon, eggs, toast and home fries—all the things you should have if you're going to eat breakfast at a diner. We'd long since given up trying to convince the other that ours was the better breakfast.

"Your sponsor says you're doing really well at school," Angel said.

I grinned. "Ah ha. Another clue. So he's someone at the university."

I already knew he was male, having ferreted that information out during a previous conversation.

Angel smiled. "Or he knows someone there."

She wasn't giving anything away anymore.

I didn't know why I felt this compulsion to play detective with my sponsor's identity. What difference did it make who he was? And what if it backfired on me? What if this was like the locked fairy tale room and as soon as I figured out who he was, everything would be taken away?

But I was born curious, as they used to say back in Tyler. I always just had to *know*. If I kept a journal or a diary, all the entries would end up being questions—and not the most sensible ones, either. As it is, I scrawled them in the margins of my sketchbooks.

What if cars ran on dog poop?
Where does dawn end and the day begin?
Why can't mice fly?

Silly questions. Questions without answers. Each with an accompanying illustration. Though sometimes the drawings had nothing to do with the words scribbled alongside them.

Written in pencil in the margin alongside a colour study rendered in soft pastels of the crystal prism hanging in the window of my room was: *Why do so many of us have to try so hard to be happy? Why, so often, does it not work?*

Or in an ink sketch of a Chinese grocery store, I'd written where the name of the store should be: *Why can't I hear colours like Davy does?* Davy being the slightly autistic son of one of Angel's clients.

I think I just needed to get things out of me—especially now, at this point in my life, when there was no one to tell me I couldn't, or I shouldn't. No parent, caseworker, policeman. No judge or pimp. There was just me.

I read an artist's statement at a group show that I went to awhile ago. She wrote: I'm small on the outside with a vast inner landscape of dreams, ideas, wishes, hopes and ideals. She could have been describing me, because the press of my inner landscape was so big that it was forever pushing at the seams of my skin. Sometimes I thought that if I didn't let some of it out, I'd just burst. So I painted and I drew, and I talked and I asked questions, and sometimes I danced like a mad dervish—alone in my room, or even on the university common.

Which wasn't to say that I was a complete chatterbox. I could listen, too. Like Christy says, everybody's got a story, and no matter what anybody tries to tell you, none of them is more important than the other. I just had to talk to Angel's clients to know how true that was. Maybe the life of some junkie wasn't of the same earthshaking relevance to the world at large as something that made the front page of the newspaper, but it overshadowed everything else in *her* life. There might be a war on in Vietnam, but that didn't have near the impact on her life as a judge kicking her sorry ass into county for a month less a day.

When we'd finished eating, Angel got that look—jonesing for a cigarette. She'd only just quit and was doing really well with it so far. To help distract her from the urge, I asked her about the case she was helping out on.

"Honestly?" she said. "I don't have a clue how it's going."

The case had echoes of Skeeter's problems. The girl was going into rehab in lieu of doing time in county. While she was in custody during the trial, her grandmother was taking care of her little boy. But things got complicated because the girl's boyfriend—who was also the boy's birth father—wanted guardianship of his son. The grandmother was fighting it, saying that since he'd been the girl's pimp and dealer, the last place her great grandson should be was with him. The boyfriend claimed he'd cleaned up his act, and besides that, he'd never pimped the boy's mother.

Word on the street said this was true, but there were holes in his story that the grandmother's lawyers were only too eager to pounce on. Because of that—because, right or wrong, the girl believed in her boyfriend—she and her grandmother had become estranged, and now the grandmother was pushing for permanent legal guardianship of her great grandson.

"My big problem," Angel said, "is that I can't fully commit to the boyfriend being completely upfront with us. This whole business is sucking away far more time than I thought it would, but I know I have to see it through."

I nodded. "Except meanwhile, a hundred other things are falling apart back at the office."

"Not quite a hundred. But more than I'd like."

"I could help out," I said.

She shook her head. "You're already stretched way too thin as it is."

"Said the kettle to the pot."

"No, I'm serious," she said. "I understand that keeping busy stops you from falling back into your own ways. I get that. I really do. But you need more than just studying and work. It wouldn't hurt to have a little bit of a social life."

"I do have a social life."

"I meant one where you're not dragging your friends to the soup kitchen, or studying together in the library—all good things," she adds before I can protest. "But what about having a little fun?"

"I have fun."

"You know what I mean."

I did, but for all her insight and smarts, she didn't get it, and I'd yet been able to convince her that all these things that kept me busy *were* my idea of fun. Anything that didn't include lying spaced out on a squat mattress, or shuffling through the streets for a fix, or blowing some guy in an alley was gold. Knowing that I could make a difference—that I could be someone different—made every day special.

"So how do you do it?" I asked her. "How do you balance it all? Maybe more to the point, *why* do you take on all you do?"

She looked out the window for a moment before returning her gaze to mine.

"Because I can," she said. "Because to do any less would be shirking my responsibilities."

"You can't be responsible for everybody."

"I know. But when I do give my word that I'll help somebody, I have to keep it. And if I see someone in need that I could help, I have to help them. No matter how busy I already am."

"And you're saying I'm stretched too thin."

"You had a crap life," she said. "And even though you're earning each and every one of them, you deserve a few breaks." She leaned forward. "It's important that you see your studies through. You need to see that you can finish things. That you can take on a commitment and fulfill it. What you do after you get your degree—that's up to you. But right now, your main responsibility is to yourself. You have to prove this to yourself."

"And you?" I asked. "What are you proving by taking on as much as you do?"

"Nothing. I just believe that everybody's got their part to play in making the world a better place. I honestly believe that, for all the people you help at the soup kitchen or St. Vincent's, your art is going to allow you to make a much bigger impact on far more people than either you or I could possibly make in the day-to-day guerilla war that I'm engaged in."

I just sat there and stared at her. She'd never mentioned this before. I knew she believed that my art was important to me. The more I did it, the more I realized it was my lifeline to everything my life hadn't been before. But I couldn't see how it could help anybody else.

"Come on," I said. "I like to paint fairies and little goblins. How's that going to mean anything to anybody else?"

"The operative word," she said, "is hope. That's what your art can bring into people's lives."

"Hope."

"Exactly. Remember Susie?"

I nodded. Twelve-year-old Susie Berman had come into Angel's care having barely survived a childhood that made my own seem like an inconvenience. The broken fingers and cigarette burn scars on her neck and the backs of her hands were only the tip of a monstrous iceberg. Angel had almost gone to jail, keeping Susie out of the clutches of her freak family, constantly shunting her around among her various friends so that the authorities couldn't track her down.

Susie had spent a few nights with me at the Chelsea and she'd been fascinated by my drawings. I still couldn't do properly proportioned human figures, and certainly couldn't back then, but my little twig fairies didn't need proper proportions to work and Susie had loved to watch me draw them. I would have tried to teach her how to do them herself, but at the time her fingers were still healing from having been slammed repeatedly in a dresser's drawers and she couldn't hold a pencil.

So evenings before she went to sleep, I'd have her direct me to draw them in various poses. The last time I'd seen her—Angel finally had her placed in a safe environment—she'd left clutching a spiral-ringed notebook filled with the drawings I'd done for her.

"God, how's she doing now?" I asked.

"All things considered, really well."

I tried to figure out what Angel was getting at by bringing her up. Yes, my little drawings had helped to amuse her while she was staying with me, but I couldn't see any larger connection to what Angel and I had just been talking about.

"That notebook with your drawings that you gave her," Angel explained, "your art. It became a talisman for her—a symbol of safety and hope. She won't go anywhere without it. I saw her the other day and she still carries it around with her."

I opened my mouth, but Angel didn't let me speak.

"Now you're going to say," she went on, "that's one little girl. And it was your presence in her life that made a difference. But I also know the art helped save her—is still saving her. Just as it could help some other person. Maybe many other persons." She paused, then added, "The way that book of fairy tales you had as a child helped save you, though you never met the author."

"Wow," was all I could say.

"Wow, indeed."

"But I still don't..."

"Your art," Angel said. "I believe that's your responsibility—the gift you bring into the world that no one else can. And I also believe that it could make a real difference—not just in one life, but in many lives."

"Wow," I said again. I studied her for a long moment. "You really believe that, don't you?"

"I really do," she told me.

"Way to put the pressure on me."

She just smiled.

-11-

I spend the afternoon and the early part of the evening just wandering, up this street, down another. I suppose I had something to eat at some point in the day because I'm not hungry, but I don't remember doing it. I know I sat and drew for awhile. I made a couple of attempts to draw Julianna, but except for the hair, I just couldn't get her right. I had better luck with a portrait of Donna—though when it was done, I realized that it was halfway between the way she looked now and how I remembered her from the old days. Still, at least I liked it.

I was tempted to tear out the two I did of Julianna, but in the end I left them in. The sketchbook is for me, chronicling the good and the bad. And the bad ones keep me honest.

I think about that, and about Rebecca Rebecca and her improvateers, and about Cholo and his niece. I think about everything except the thing that should be most on my mind: the fact that I'm stuck here.

I'm good at that. I'm good at putting the things I don't want to think about in little boxes and sinking them somewhere deep in my brain. I've done it since I was a little girl. It's how I get through the day.

When I don't have drugs.

But while there are some things you can bury away forever, being stuck here is still happening and eventually I have to go back to trying to figure out what I'm going to do.

No, that's a lie. I know what I'm going to have to do—I just don't want to do it.

I have to see Julianna again and let her send that shadow of me back. I know it's wrong, but I have to weigh that against the promises I made back home—those implicit, and those assumed.

And maybe it won't be so bad.

This shadow…

Something that didn't have a life will now get a chance at having one. Maybe she'll surprise me—if I could be there to see it. Maybe she'll be strong and be true to her friends. Maybe she'll stay clean, graduate, make a name for herself. Maybe she won't make such an awful mess of her life the way I did.

No, that's not right. She'll have experienced everything I have up until Julianna pulls her out of me and sends her back to the world of the living, so she'll have to carry the same baggage of history that I do.

I wonder if it'll hurt.

Probably.

How could it not? How could you get rid of pieces of yourself—even if they're ones you don't want—and not feel the loss?

I sit up and look around myself. I don't know when it got dark, but it is. Dark, and everything's quiet. It's just me, out in the night again. I don't mind the dark or the night, even if nobody else in this city seems to like it, but I realize I'm too close to the canal, so I get up and walk in the opposite direction from it. The voices have been coming back, echoing inside my head. They're just a murmur at the moment, a mumble that I can't quite make out. I'm pretty sure if I get too close to the canal they'll reawaken full-blown in my head again.

I don't recognize this part of the city, but if what Gus says is true, that's hardly surprising. I guess you could spend your whole life travelling around in it and always find something new—new being a relative term for a place where nothing really seems to change.

I'm walking down the middle of a street, fearless because there's no traffic. I try to decide if I should call Julianna now, or wait until morning. I can't see how it'd make much difference either way. Now, later, the shadow will still get to go back and I'll still be stuck here.

I walk over to the sidewalk and sit on a bench at a bus stop. There are no buses running, of course. I don't wear a watch, so I have no idea what time it is.

"It's a little past midnight," a voice says from beside me and I get a real understanding of what it feels like to jump out of your skin.

I don't do it literally, mind you, but I do jump up from the bench, my pulse leaping into overtime. I have my hand at my throat as I turn to see who spoke.

The girl sitting there in bell-bottom jeans and a black T gives me an amused look. She appears perfectly harmless—a little taller than me, probably, with straight black hair and pale, pale features that I decide are exaggerated by the raccoon make-up around her eyes and the dark slash of her lipstick. She lifts a hand to push some loose hair back from her face. Her nails are painted black.

"God, you gave me a scare," I say as I sit back down.

"Are you sure it was me?" she asks. "Maybe you just have a guilty conscience."

"What's that supposed to—" I break off as something else occurs to me. "How'd you know I was wondering what time it was?"

She shrugs and gives me a grin. "Maybe I can read your mind."

"Oh, yeah? What am I thinking right now?"

"That it's nice to have someone to talk to?"

That wasn't what I was thinking of, but she's right all the same. Having someone to talk to means I don't have to think. It means I can put off calling Julianna for a little longer.

"I'm Jilly," I say and offer her my hand.

"Lovely."

Her handshake is strong, her skin cool to the touch.

"So what's your name?" I ask.

"I just told you. I'm Lovely." She smiles. "Or at least that's the name I'm trying on tonight." She cocks her head and adds, "Though maybe I need to grow into it."

What an odd thing to say, I think, but I let myself fall into her playful mood.

"Maybe," I tell her. "But you might want to wear a dress and lose those shoes. I usually think of something lovely as being all light and graceful."

Under the wide cuff of her bell-bottoms, she's wearing a pair of clunky shoes that look more suitable for a workman.

"Good point," she says.

We sit there for a few moments, looking at the empty street in front of us.

"So," I say, "how come you're not hidden away at home like everybody else is at night?"

She turns to look at me and shrugs. "I like the night."

"Me, too. But I thought there was a curfew or something to keep people off the streets after dark."

"I don't think so. I think people here just have such full days that they don't have any energy left by the time the night rolls around."

"Someone told me it's like Disneyland," I say. "That an army of little gnomes and goblins run around and make sure everything is ship-shape in time for the next day."

"What a fun idea."

"I guess. But I've been out every night and, so far? Completely free of little fairy people."

"Maybe they're invisible."

"I hadn't thought of that."

"Or maybe someone was pulling your leg." She waits a beat, then asks, "So why are you sitting at a bus stop when the bus won't arrive until morning?"

Now it's my turn to shrug. "I don't have anywhere else to be."

She looks surprised. "You don't have a place to stay?"

"Oh, I've got a nice apartment and everything. It's to die for, really—though I didn't have to."

I give her a look, hoping I haven't made some faux pas. I'm still not sure if people object being reminded how they got here. And then...

I don't know when it happened, but I suddenly realize that she's different. The punky hippie look is gone. She's wearing a sleeveless dress now—it's a pale ivory with a satiny sheen—and her clunky shoes have become elegant lace-up boots. She seems a few years older, too, and her make-up is much more subtle.

"What...how...?

I clear my throat and try starting again.

"Who...who are you?" I ask.

She just smiles for a long moment, but then she says, "I am the night sky when the stars are dreaming. I am the subway car, sleeping deep underground. I am the birdsong at dawn that only the foxes hear. I am the highest flagpole, on the tallest building, and I am the flag, too, fluttering in the wind."

"Mireya," I say. "That's who you are. You're Mireya, aren't you?"

She cocks her head. "Now who gave you that name?"

I remember Julianna saying something about how she can come and go from this world to any number of others. Considering how Mireya makes people stay here, she probably wouldn't like someone being able to do that. She'd probably stop her.

"What does it matter?" I say. "I'm either right or wrong. Which is it?"

"You are a forthright young woman, aren't you?"

When she calls me "young woman," I realize she's changed again. She's older still, in her forties now. Her hair's shorter, her slim figure more filled out. The sleek, satin dress has become a more durable linen, but the cut is still exquisite.

"I just like to know who I'm talking to," I say.

"Names are for people—the living and the dead. We…I and my sisters and my brothers…we don't have the same need for names as you do. They're too much like labels."

"But nevertheless, convenient. So I'll think of you as Mireya until you tell me different."

Yes, I'm being—what did she call it? Forthright. But I'm putting on a much braver front than the way I feel inside, which is all panicked and quivery. But you have to do that with those who are stronger than you. You can't show your weakness or they'll walk all over you. Mireya will probably do that anyway—there's something mocking in her tone when she talks to me, like everything about me amuses her, but as soon as I stop being amusing she'll…I don't know. Erase me or something.

"So what else did your informant tell you?" she asks.

"Um…that I can't go back to my own world…."

"That much is true."

"But that a piece of me can."

She studies me for a moment, then nods.

"Yes," she says. "I see you still have your shadow."

I take a breath to steady my nerve, then plunge ahead.

"Look, I just want to go home," I tell her.

"No one is here who hasn't chosen to be here."

"I know a grumpy old man named Gus who'd argue with you about that."

She smiles. "Oh, him. Don't let him take you in with his stories. When he was alive he worked in a large office, always doing what he was told, always saying, yes sir, no sir. He wants to be cantankerous. He likes to play the devil's advocate."

"Is there really a devil?"

She shrugs. "I don't know, but why not? Why can't everything you imagine be out there, somewhere?"

I know I started us on this digression, and I have to admit that a part of me finds it interesting, but I have to focus on what I need from her.

"So can I imagine myself being back home?"

She shakes her head. "Everybody else is happy here—why can't you be happy, too?"

"Because I'm not supposed to be here. It was just a fluke that I ever crossed over."

"Why are you so sure about that? I know you better than you might imagine, just as I know all my charges. Everything you've ever wanted is here. It's a place of safety. A place filled with magic."

I can't tell you how much it creeps me out that she says she knows me so well. Especially when she's right. Because I do want to be safe. And I love the idea of magic. But not like this. Not pretend. If I'm going to have either in my life, they need to be real.

"They are real," she says, reading my mind again, I guess. "Everyone who comes here finds their heart's desire waiting for them. I give you what you want, and you, in turn, nourish me through how you live your lives."

"What, you're like some kind of vampire?"

She gives me a disappointed look. "Hardly. I only gain satisfaction from your happiness."

"Except," I say, as I consider what she's telling me, "the people that died to get here. Aren't you stopping them from going on to—I don't know, where we're supposed to go when we die?"

"How do you know this isn't one aspect of that very destination?"

"I don't, I guess."

"And remember: everyone has a choice. I force no one."

"Me, being the exception."

"No, you decided. When you accepted the apartment, and accepted the bank account, and began to make your new life here."

I shake my head. I want to say something, to tell her she's wrong, but she's studying me and her scrutiny is so intense, that every part of me feels tight and tense. It's like my skin's shrinking.

"One of my sisters has touched you," she says. "I see a great light in you. But I see a great darkness, too."

Her face softens and I feel like I can breathe again. Her gaze meets mine with warmth.

"Don't be in such a hurry to leave," she tells me. "This place is a much better world for you. If you were to go back, you'd have to always fight for the smallest victories."

"But that's just it," I say. "I've only just learned that I can fight. That I am strong enough to make it on my own. Please, don't make me beg. Don't make me send my shadow back to take my place."

She shakes her head. "Your shadow couldn't do that. It can go back, but it wouldn't have your light."

"I don't care about any stupid light. I just want to go home."

I see something change in her eyes, and just like that, I can tell that she's bored with me. Bored with me and with this conversation.

She stands up from the bench and looks down at me until I stand up, too. Then she surprises me.

"I will think about this," she says.

"Please. Can't you decide now—"

And just like that, she's way taller than she was. Stern, with angry lights flashing in her eyes.

"Don't try my patience," she tells me. "I'm not some flighty little spirit who will give in because, oh, you're so sad that you're not getting your way."

"I'm sorry, I just—"

"I said I will think about it. But now you must go back to your apartment—the apartment I was kind enough to provide you with. Go there and wait."

"Sure. I just—"

"Not another word."

"Okay. You win. I'm going."

Is she reading my mind right now? Because I'll do what she says. I'll go back to the apartment. But then I'm going to see about sending my shadow back. Light or no light, at least it'll be able to see my friends and make things right with them.

At least a piece of me will be free.

"You are an obstinate young woman," she says.

And then...then...

She's standing there, looming over me. I don't know where she got the cloak. The hood is pushed back and her face is round and pale as a full moon. Something moves in the cloak—not her arms and legs. There's too much motion—everywhere, pushing the fabric in too many directions. The full moon becomes an owl's face. The cloak falls away and crumples to the ground. Her body...she...

A flock of birds erupts from the cloak. The fabric falls to the ground, pooling in a dark crumple of cloth. The birds circle once around me, led by the owl that had been her face. Then they all fly off in a thunder of wings, across the street, up above the building on the other side.

I stand there for a long time after they're gone. It's so quiet. It's quiet everywhere. On the street and in my head. Then slowly I start to walk. I don't pick any particular direction. I know that whatever direction I take, I'll find myself on the street where my apartment is.

When I finally get back, I sit up in the windowseat and stare out at the night. I know I could go upstairs and see Donna and Tommy, but I just want to be alone. I'm trying to make sense of everything I just saw and heard, but I can't seem to keep my thoughts in one place. I'm not ready to call for Julianna, either.

I will think about this, the spirit said.

Did that mean she might send me back?

She kept changing so much. Funny and sweet, then so stern.

Go there and wait.

And those birds.

She became a flock of birds.

I feel myself completely unraveling, so I do the only thing that ever seems to calm me now. I do it when I'm overwhelmed. When the jones hits hard and I'm all alone at night in my little room back in Newford. Just like I'm all alone right now.

I pull my sketchbook from my pocket and I start to draw.

A flock of birds.

In the shape of a woman.

And at some point I get so tired that I lie down on the bed and I fall asleep, my sketchbook still clutched in my hands.

Knocking on the door wakes me the next morning.

I sit up, bleary and unprepared to see anybody. The knocking is repeated. I find myself holding my sketchbook and I put it aside as I get up and go to the door.

"Good morning," Geordie says with relentless good cheer.

I feel hungover, but I don't remember going out drinking. It's just not something I do anymore. I have a beer now and again, but I never drink enough to get tipsy, and I never get drunk. Not anymore. Those days are gone.

Geordie hands me a Styrofoam cup.

"You look like you need this," he says.

I muster a smile—it's hard not to smile when Geordie's in a good mood—and take the cup from him.

"I have croissants as well," he says, holding up a paper bag that's stained with grease on the bottom.

"Don't put that down on anything," I tell him.

I go to find a newspaper. There's one on the floor by the chair. I drop it on the bed and he puts the bag on it. Then we sit on either end of the bed, the bag between us. We drink coffee. We eat delicious croissants.

"These are fabulous," I say around a bite that melts in my mouth. "You must be flush if you sprang for the real thing."

"We brought in such a good crowd last night that the club owner gave us each an extra ten bucks."

"So it was a good gig?"

"One of the best. You should have come."

I think of an evening of fiddling and lively songs.

"I should have," I tell him.

"So what did you do last night?" he asks. "Was the club there?"

"The club?"

"Where your friend was playing. What was it called again? Cool Hand Luke's?"

I shake my head. "Cool Hand's Juke. No, I…"

I look around my room.

"You know what?" I say. "I think I just fell asleep and never got out. No wonder I'm feeling so groggy. I must have slept for—what time is it?"

"Nine-thirty."

"God. I think I slept for fourteen hours."

"You're lucky I came by to wake you up. Otherwise, you'd have languished away in here without food or drink until you became just a shadow of yourself."

Shadow of myself. The words echo in my head. Why do they creep me out the way they do? It's just an expression. But it makes me feel…I don't know. Hazy and thin. Like I'm not all here.

"But you must have needed the sleep," Geordie says.

I nod in agreement. "Must have."

He grins. "So now we'll never know."

"Know what?"

"If the club exists."

"Of course it exists."

Geordie smiles. "Of course it does."

The weird feeling I had a moment ago fades away. I smile back at him. I don't know why, but I feel inordinately pleased to see him this morning.

-12-

Newford, 1973

I t's Halloween night and Wendy's having a party at her place. Actually it's just an excuse for her to get to meet this guy she's been crushing on, but none of us mind. We like getting together, and we like seeing our friends happy in love.

But before I go to her place, I have an errand to run. Maybe it's crazy—I don't know. If I told anybody I was coming here—and why—they'd think I was crazy. Truth to tell, I think I might be a little crazy, too, but here I am, all the same, standing at the corner of Norton and Flood.

I look at the watch Sophie gave me a couple of weeks ago and check the time. Watches never work for her, but she keeps buying them all the same, and then ends up giving them away. She has this problem with technology—I told her she should call her problem Jinx and make friends with it, then maybe it would be nicer to her. Anyway, if something has electronics, or gears—or any kind of mechanical or electrical parts—it pretty much doesn't work for her. Watches run backward, radios play weird stations, her phone rings when there's no one there, or it's someone talking to her in Japanese, or Flemish.

But the watch works just fine for me.

I don't believe anything's going to happen, but I study the street anxiously all the same. I feel like there's too much traffic, but it's not like I can do anything about it. All I can do is stare out across the pavement and worry.

And then it happens.

I honestly thought it wouldn't. I honestly thought that this obsession I had about coming out here on this day, at this time, was my own Jinx—just a weird mix-up in my DNA that left me with this improbable compulsion.

But there she is, in the middle of the street.

Donna.

Lying there on the pavement, like a body laid out on a gurney.

Which is what she was, all those years ago when she got multiple stab wounds in county and ended up dying in an ambulance on the way to the hospital.

A car screeches its brakes as she sits up. The car's going too fast to stop, so the driver whips into the next lane, cutting off a cab with inches to spare. The cabbie leans on his horn, but I'm no longer paying attention. My gaze is riveted on my dead friend as she scrambles to her feet and darts across the intersection, almost getting hit by another car in the process.

She's on the opposite side of the street from me. I keep my gaze on her as I wait for the light to change. I'm halfway across the intersection before she notices me, her eyes going comically wide.

She's not the Donna I remember from the Home for Wayward Girls, or from my junkie days. She's the Donna I thought I'd dreamed up: punky, with a Bettie Page haircut and a swatch of tattoos running down either arm. I know there are more of them on her chest and back, but she's wearing a leather vest and I can't see them.

She just stares at me as I finish crossing the street and walk up to her.

"Hey, Donna," I say.

I am so loving this moment. Partly because it means I'm not crazy. But mostly because now I get the chance to spend a day with Donna who, for this one day, isn't dead anymore.

"I wasn't sure you'd come," I add.

She's still just looking at me. Finally she reaches out and touches my shoulder.

"How come you remember?" she says. "Better yet, how did you ever get back? I've been hoping that's what happened, but I had no clue. That's why I came today—to find out."

"Well, you've answered one question that's been bothering me," I say. "For the past year, I was never sure if it was really me who came back, or my shadow."

"This is just too weird."

I smile. "What? No hug?"

We embrace and hold each other tightly for a long moment. When we step apart, I take her arm.

"Let's go find some place quiet where we can talk," I say.

She nods. "Yeah, talking would be good."

There's a diner down the street and we take a window booth. Donna immediately flips through the song selection on the little jukebox at the end of our table.

"I don't know half these bands," she says. "Where's all the rockabilly music?"

"It's 1973," I tell her. "Things are different."

"I'll say."

The waitress brings us each a coffee and Donna loads hers up with three spoons of sugar and double cream.

"So how come you're here?" she asks. "I mean, I know it's to see me, but how come you remember?"

I take one of the two sketchbooks I'm carrying out of my knapsack. The one I leave inside is my current book. The one I push across the table to her I found on my bed the morning Geordie woke me with coffee and croissants. The morning after I was supposed to have gone to meet Donna at a club that I later found out didn't exist.

Except it did. Or it had. For one night.

Donna opens the sketchbook and starts to flip through the pages. She smiles then, recognizing the subjects of many of the drawings.

"I don't remember," I say when her gaze lifts up to meet mine. "Not most of the time. But when I'm holding that sketchbook, and especially when I look at the drawings I did…that's when I do. But if I put it away on a shelf, it all just slides away again, right out of my mind."

"I forgot," she says. "You were always drawing over there."

I nod. "And for some reason, the drawings came back with me."

"So how'd you get back?"

"I'm not really sure."

I tell her about my last night there, in her world. She listens, but she keeps flipping through the sketchbook. She pauses at one page and puts her finger on a couple of lines I've wrote on it. They're right under the portrait I did of her, the last night I was in that other world:

> *Go to the corner of Norton and Flood on Halloween.*
>
> *Find out the exact time she died.*
>
> *Be there at that time!!!!*

"How'd you find out the time?" she asks. "Or have you been waiting all day?"

I shake my head. "It wasn't hard. My friend Angel has connections with the ambulance company." I smile. "Truth is, I think she has connections everywhere."

"And so you came here to see me."

"Thinking I was crazy the whole time."

"God, this is so amazing."

I laugh. "You think it's amazing?"

We just look at each other or a long moment, grinning like a pair of fools.

"So did you make the right choice?" she asks. "Are you happy here?"

"Mostly. It's hard. But I feel like anything I accomplish, I've earned. That's a great feeling for a Carter out of Hillbilly Holler."

"Except you're not a Carter anymore."

I nod. "Remember how we used to pretend that we didn't really belong to the families we came from? How there had to have been some kind of mix-up at the hospital when we were born?"

Now it's her turn to nod.

"That feels like the true story now."

"Then I'm happy for you."

"And what about you? Are you still in your band? How's Tommy?"

Her eyes cloud briefly, but then she gives me a bright smile that I can see right through. I reach across the table and take her hand.

"What happened?" I ask.

"He went on."

"Went on where?"

"I don't know. Wherever people go next, I guess. He...he loved being with me, J.C. I know that. But he was a lot like you. He just didn't feel like he was supposed to be there. And then one morning I woke up early and I just knew the apartment was empty."

"Mireya told me that no one had to stay in the city unless they wanted to," I say. "I guess she let him go, just like she did with me."

"I guess."

I squeeze her hand. "So are you okay?"

She shrugs. "Yes and no. I'm thinking...I'm thinking of going myself. I don't exactly know how you're supposed to do it. I guess you just let go or something."

"Oh, Donna..."

"No, it's cool. I mean, I feel weird, and I miss the both of you like crazy—you and Tommy—but that's not why. I just feel like I'm ready or something."

"I wrecked everything for you, didn't I?"

She shakes her head. "No, you opened my eyes. The city's great for some people. And it was great for me for awhile. But I need to move on. I might have tried to go on sooner, but I needed to come here first. To see you. To make sure you really got back okay."

"I did. But I still feel—"

"Up for some shenanigans, I hope."

She's grinning again, and though there's something wistful, hiding in her eyes, I know she's mostly in good spirits. She's always been like that. I was always the worrier and the brooder, but I've changed. Because a lot of the time, if you act like you're happy, this funny thing happens and you actually start to feel happy.

I learned that from her.

"Because," she says, "I'm not going to spend this last night with you moping when we could be having fun."

I think of my friends, waiting for me at Wendy's. I would so love to share them with Donna.

"Are you up for a party?" I ask.